Evelyn Pyne

**A Dream of the Gironde**

And other Poems

Evelyn Pyne

**A Dream of the Gironde**
*And other Poems*

ISBN/EAN: 9783337158347

Printed in Europe, USA, Canada, Australia, Japan

Cover: Foto ©Andreas Hilbeck / pixelio.de

More available books at **www.hansebooks.com**

# A

# DREAM OF THE GIRONDE

A

# DREAM OF THE GIRONDE

*AND OTHER POEMS*

BY

EVELYN PYNE

LONDON

SMITH, ELDER, & CO., 15 WATERLOO PLACE

1877

TO

THE DEAR MEMORY OF HER

WHO

DEAD TO THE WORLD

BLOOMS A STAR IN MY HEART FOR EVER

# CONTENTS.

A

# DREAM OF THE GIRONDE

# CHARACTERS.

ROLAND  
BUZOT  
BARBAROUX  
PÉTION } *Girondists.*  
BRISSOT  
VERGNIAUD  
LOUVET  

DANTON  
ROBESPIERRE } *Montagnards, at first friends of the* Gironde.  
CAMILLE DESMOULINS  
CHAMFORT  

S. HURUGE  
ROSSIGNOL } *Violent revolutionists.*  
JOURDAIN  
LEGENDRE  

LOUIS, *King of France.*  
RAOUL.  
PRESIDENT OF TRIBUNAL.  
MADAME ROLAND, *wife to* Roland.  
MARIE, *her child.*  
MARIE ANTOINETTE, *Queen of France.*  
*Her two* children.  
MADAME ELIZABETH, *sister to* Louis.  
PRINCESSE DE LAMBALLE.  
MADAME BONCHAUD, *jailor's wife.*  
THÉROIGNE DE MÉRICOURT, *a violent revolutionist betrayed and deserted by* Raoul.  

| | |
|---|---|
| Nurse to Marie. | Executioner. |
| Beggar. | Jailor. |
| Old Man. | Various citizens. |
| Public Accuser. | Officers. |

SCENE.—*In and near Paris.*

# ACT I.

### MADAME ROLAND.

The years roll back, and I again am young :
A merry child, yet thoughtful 'midst my glee,
And bearing still about me a faint trace
Of heaven, I left with tears—and a dim glance
(They tell me) of that heaven in pensive eyes,
And brow attuned to wonder, and low voice,
Which ever knocked at hearts, and craved a place—
In joy or sorrow,—only just a place,—
A little niche—a cranny—there to rest—
Nor feel alone in this wide earth of tears.
And still that feeling lives, and still it leads
Me from the abstract to the personal :
I feel the urging of my woman soul
Against the man's strong will, which must endure
Tho' cast from kindred hearts, and all alone
Forced to toil on ; a blessing, but unbless'd :
Until death lifts the curtain, and men feel
What they could never see, and know too late
The God's gift, which they counted all too poor
For little human love to rest upon ! . . . .
My God, Thou knowest that my soul is set,

B 2

Firm as the earth, upon my country's weal ;
Thou knowest that from youth, my every thought
Was but a seeking of that narrow path
Prepared for each, and leading through the grave
Straight onward to the stars :—and now at last
The way seems clear ;—the power is in my hands ;
Yet these weak woman hands delay to grasp,
And tremble at the treasure !   I could cast
The costly bauble down, and never sigh
If . . . .(ah these 'ifs !' the woman's weakness—fault—
Misfortune—what you will—they ever come,)
In one heart I might reign :—but this is sin,
Not merely weakness ; does it spring, alas,
From sweetness in my mother, whose meek heart,
Tho' hidden, still returns in me, her child ?
Ah Mother, early lost but ne'er forgot,
Is it your gentle spirit that draws near
When most I feel the woman ?   Bless me now,
Oh spirit ! bless me : for I am thy child,
Tho' different, yet thine own : and I still feel
That longing to gain entrance in each heart
Around me (ah ! the woman's weakness still :)
The one, and not the many ; the dear one,
And not the suffering many ; the one love
Is thought of, prayed for, kissed, and yet (ah me !)
The many are passed o'er with careless glance
Or mutter'd benediction :—I pray God
To tear this woman heart away from me—
Destroy all merely personal loving,
And take away this thirsting for one heart,
My mother's gift, my sweet dead mother's gift :—
For detail was to her as daily bread,

Or morning draught of water ; she would miss
The level sunlight slanting o'er the plain,
Embracing mountain peaks with holy kiss,
And lighting forests with the mystic glow
Of o'er entwinèd branches, whose dim shade
A woven emerald darkness half concealed,
And half (enraptured) sighed to full display ;
To watch the truant beam on leaf or flower :
Perhaps she lost the star-glow (who can say ?)
In groping for stellaria ; yet her life
Passed bless'd and blessing, out of human ken,
And left a fragrance, faint and tender still,
A perfume like the passing monthly rose
Or fragile mignonette :—and I her child
Have echoes of her nature, and look back
From glory—freedom—to a humble home,
And quiet joys, with something of regret :
I would not that 'twere possible to change
My visions into truth ; yet there are hours
When life seems all too hard—joy all too brief—
And dreams a sweet reality ! There love
Springs in a moment fire-winged unto heaven,
And pierces the empyrean—there my soul
Needs no support, and Liberty my god,
And goddess, (for no sex is there, but full
Of both, yet neither, reigns as both in one,)
Comes to me crowned, triumphant : then indeed
I am content, yes then—yet some slight thing—
A voice—the merest trifle—breaks my dream
And drags me down to life, then—then I long,
In weakness of the flesh, for but one hour
Of joy, were death the end, that I might taste

One second of life's wine, then dash the cup
For ever into fragments.   But enough
Of these vain foolish thoughts—actions not dreams
Are now my part ; and I feel strong and firm,
If need, to grasp the sword—the sword of death.
Have I not read of Romans till their soul
Hath entered into mine ?   Away regrets !
No selfish dreams of happiness for me ;
My country is my love, and shall be served
As I would serve my lover—unto death !

---

## SCENE II.

*Enter* BUZOT.

MADAME ROLAND.

Good morrow friend, bring you good news? (*anxiously*)
    but no,
You look too grave for fortune.

BUZOT.

               Is it so ?
Then ask no further ; bad news wing their way
Too quickly ever—let me choose I pray
The subject of our speech.

MADAME ROLAND (*gazing earnestly at him*).

               Of course 'twill be
Our country's happiness and liberty ;
No other theme befits the time, and thee.
Speak on then, Buzot, ever true and free.

BUZOT.

Our country's happiness ! yes, that's our aim;
Yet what is happiness except a name ?
Can it be found ?   I doubt it.

MADAME ROLAND (*passionately*).

                                  Happiness !
We seek for happiness instead of truth ;
We choose out pleasure, and ignore the right,
Then call life dark : eternity will judge
If darkness be not shadow of ourselves
O'ercasting all—our love—our hope—our life !
Self must be blotted out—a thing of naught—
Forgotten—non-existent, ere we catch
The light which our life holds, but does not hide
From those who truly seek.          [*Taking his hand*;
                             Oh friend, be strong
Forget thyself, and thine own petty griefs,
Think of thy country, think on Liberty !
Strive not for thine own happiness—in vain—
It will elude thee even to the end ;—
But set thyself apart from all mankind
In some wild spot, where Nature only dwells,
And looking deeply into thine own soul
(No thought of self to darken, or deceive),
Tell over all thy dreams, and hopes and aims,
From thy youth upwards,—and then choose the one
Which seemeth best to thee (for thou art great
In thine own heart, and hast not left the shore
Of youth so long, but echoes float across
From heaven hovering o'er our infancy).

Thine aim once fixed, pursue it unto death.
Be gracious to thy friends, loving to all,
Patient and brave ; but ever follow on
To thy ideal.   Wilt thou find life dark ?
I tell thee no ; this, thine aim, being high,
High as the stars which shine above us still,
The very strife to near, and reach, will bring
Light to thy path, and thou wilt truly feel
Life's object—noble aims accomplishèd.
                    [*She drops his hand and half turns away.*

### BUZOT.

My guardian angel ! heaven speaks by thee.
I will obey ; and yet, before I flee,
One question more : in this thine own bright way
Oh, art thou happy ? tell me this, I pray.

### MADAME ROLAND (*dreamily*).

Happy ?—I happy ?—yes : I think I'm so.
Yet what is happiness ? does one not know
When one feels bright, or gay, or sad, or ill ?
But happy ?—ah that cannot be, until
The depths of misery are left behind,
The world's deep scorn—hatred of friends unkind,—
An empty heart, where love has always been,—
A hideous wreck, where bright hopes bloomed unseen—
No change, or chance of change to mar or cure,
Simply a dull hard blank :—this to endure
As in a dream, and then to wake and find
It was not real—a phantom of the mind
Or something less, and that we live and love,
Have joy on earth, and hope of bliss above,

And that the longings of our inmost soul
Are realised,—that we have reached the goal
Our spirit pined for ; and the heart that still
Had loved, believed, and soothed us in the ill
Now shared the good, and made our perfect bliss
If possible more perfect ; as a kiss
Seals and confirms the love—' yes ' whispered low
By bashful maid, and he who feared the ' no,'
That knell to his fair hopes, now smiles serene,
Nor cares to think how lately doubt had been
His happiest state ; he hardly dared to rest
His love on her, yet found her aye the best ;
Whether she smiled, or frowned, or passed him by
With but averted glance of her blue eye,
Or o'er him cast it scornful—still she seemed
The future queen, of whose love he had dreamed :
And now he knows her so ; the coming years
May bring him peace, or pass in bitter tears,
He heeds not ; for the present glowing joy
Is now enough :—and like the enamoured boy
I too, would say ' enough :' I know not why
I feel to-day that I could gladly die,
A coward thought; and yet—and yet—it comes—
    (*Drums and trampling of many feet heard in the
    distance.*)
Hark ! hear you not the sound of music—drums,
And many voices, and the myriad tread
Of our brave brothers, wakened from the dead,
And ready to lay down their lives, and fight
For ever for fair freedom, and the right?

BUZOT.

I go to join and lead them ; so farewell.
May happiness be yours ! I cannot tell
If it be worth the having (*aside*), but I know
I leave all hope behind me when I go. [*Exit* BUZOT.

(*Voices heard chanting as they march.*)

Brothers, let us on,
Till our fight be won ;
Liberty before us—
Justice watching o'er us.
March ! let us march ! have no fear !
If we die, we are free, shed no tear.

Kings who would enslave
Fall before the brave,
Traitors who would sell
Swift are sent to hell.
March ! let us march ! have no fear !
If we die, we are free, shed no tear.

MADAME ROLAND (*as the last words are wafted to her ear*).

' March ! let us march ! have no fear ! '
Ah friends, my countrymen, may I still hear
That soul-inspiring song, while I have breath,
And if it may be 'mid the shades of death,
(That everlasting sleep) that mortal sound
Can pierce the stillness, may its notes resound
And glad me midst my slumbers.

## SCENE III.

ROLAND (*enters hastily*).

MADAME ROLAND.

                            Bring you news ?
ROLAND.

Aye, weighty ones ; the king does now refuse
To recognise us, ministers : and we
Are cast again into the surging sea
Of citizens.

MADAME ROLAND.

            Rejoice ! 'tis better so !
'Twas with misgiving heart I saw you go
Unto that traitor's palace ; tho' I knew
The honour Liberty would gain thro' you,
And felt all the swift rapture of a choice
Which sought you out, the people's chosen voice
And Liberty's—But now there opens fair
A path for our Republic.

ROLAND.

                        I declare
Your burning words inspire me.   When I left
The palace spurned, and of the title reft
The nation had forced on me, I did think
Our cause half lost, and trembling on the brink
Of ruin all our projects ; I perceive,
Since your words fell, there is no cause to grieve,
But rather joy ; our comrades follow me ;
We will receive them now : the people see

With grand approving eye our meetings here
In freedom's cause : tyrants have all to fear
When patriots are united.

---

### SCENE IV.

*Enter* ROBESPIERRE.

ROBESPIERRE (*with great excitement*).

　　　　　　　Are you friend
Still, Roland?　We have reached the end
Of life, and may give up and die.
Is my head upon my shoulders
Still? faith I hardly know—but hark—
I hear them after us—alas !
The tyrant's butchers !　Can you hide
Me here?　You hesitate—ah where
　　　　　　　[ *gazing anxiously round the room.*
Shall I find refuge ?　I can hear
Them now, they climb the stairs—I'm lost.
　　　　　　　[*Slips behind a curtain.*

---

### SCENE V.

*Enter* BUZOT, BARBAROUX, CAMILLE DESMOULINS,
*etc. speaking hurriedly.*

BARBAROUX.

The Marseillais are here ! the people shout
For their brave Roland, and he must come out

And show himself; they think the traitor king
Has murdered him perhaps—hark how they sing !

[*The* MARSEILLAISE *heard chanted by hundreds of
voices, people shouting, drums beating, etc.*

Tremblez tyrans et vous perfides,

[MADAME ROLAND *overpowered by enthusiasm seizes
her husband's hand and rushes out into the bal-
cony singing the continuation.*

Tout est soldat pour vous combattre,
S'ils tombent.

PEOPLE (*shouting*).

They shall not fall—hurrah for Roland !
Down with the traitor Louis !
Perish all aristocrats !
Down with the tyrant!
Hurrah ! hurrah ! hurrah !

1ST CITIZEN.

Liberty !  Liberty ! for ever !

2ND CITIZEN.

Fraternity !  Eternal brotherhood !

3RD CITIZEN.

Equality ! down with everybody !
Hurrah ! hurrah ! hurrah !

PEOPLE (*all together*).

Liberty, Fraternity, Equality, for evermore!

MARSEILLAISE (*continuing*).

Marchons, qu'un sang impur, &c.

[*Gradually dies away.*

---

### SCENE VI.

ROBESPIERRE *within the room, coming from behind the curtain.*

ROBESPIERRE (*aside*).

Why all this shout of Roland? who is he?
Why not for Robespierre?   Seems to me
This people is most brutish in its taste ;
But still time goes, and slowly or with haste
My hour comes : the people shout for him,
And link his name with Liberty's blest hymn :
That tune shall change—I feel it shall.   It must.
And she, this priestess, whom we all entrust
With our religion, she shall bow to me,
Whom now she scorns, to me and Liberty.
(*Aloud.*)   Dear friends, we have been rescued once
     again,
To live for Liberty; yet 'twere no pain,
Methinks, to die for her.

CAMILLE (*aside*).

                    Nay, 'twere great gain
If thou alone could'st die !   The coward, slave
To his own vanity.

(*Aloud sneeringly.*)    Dear friend, how brave
You lately have become !   Are you certain
You felt no qualms of fear 'neath that curtain?
Or did you fight a foe ?   Since walls have ears,
Perhaps they too have swords !
  [*Exit* ROBESPIERRE, *casting at him a malignant
  glance, but saying nothing.*

---

## SCENE VII.

MADAME ROLAND *and* CAMILLE ; *in another part of the
room* BARBAROUX *and* ROLAND, *bending attentively
over maps and marking them.*

### CAMILLE.

     There goes a friend
I would were bitterest foe, for then I dare
Unmask him, and in the clear eye of day
Show forth his vileness : morning, noon, and night,
Where'er we meet, or our blest watchword sounds,
That man's malignant eye is tracking us
To our destruction, while his raven voice
Is ever croaking ' Danger! danger! danger!'

### MADAME ROLAND.

Oh speak not thus ! believe me, that man's life
Is one long sobbing gasp ' suspicion :'
'Tis a defect of nature, and must be
(As 'tis by nature) pardoned : for he has
The strongest claims upon us, freedom's love,
And weakness, which is anguish in her cause.
Oh friend, we can but struggle 'gainst our hearts,

Nor ever wholly conquer! Some have souls
Which Romanly can strive for Roman aims;
While some (alas! and this our friend is one)
Can truly see their high aims from afar,
And longing still, yet ever stumble on
Against one hindrance. Trifles to the rest
To them are mountains, and the smallest stone
Appears a rock which blots out the fair skies.
Yet Nature pardons him, and showers down
The creature-loves upon him; sister, wife,
All simple sweet home ties do fetter him—
Then surely we can suffer him, my friend.

ROLAND.

Yes: mark the boundary here, Barbaroux;
From Auvergne mountains, straight unto the sea,
For our Republic! We will bid farewell
To fickle Paris, ever surging o'er
With new requirements ere the old are won,
And with as many changes as a woman
While still within her teens. And you are sure
You know this southern people, that their heart
Keeps ever time with ours; that tyrant kings,
Or treacherous ministers, suspicious friends,
Or grasping populace can never mar
The law of Liberty, and make her reign
The anarch's boast? 'Tis hard, tho', thus to leave
Our dearly tended hopes, and quit this place,
The pride of Europe, and the earth's bright eye:
Where aught of genius, beauty, still has birth,
And shines thro' the world's darkness! Yes—'tis
    hard.

BARBAROUX.

It is our only chance, unless Fate turns
Her Janus-face again.   Let's hope she will;
But if she does not, there are hearts as brave,
Souls genius-winged, and faces bright as here,
In my fair South.   Ah, country of my heart!
Who would not love thee?   Certain, I thy son
Adore thee as the first, the blessedest,
And most deserving land for Liberty
To dwell and reign in, as in thy sons' hearts
She ever has, thro' life, thro' death, thro' hell !
Good-bye, my friend ; a few short days will prove
If Paris or the South shall shine thro' time
With ever-brightening glory, as the throne
Of Freedom, chased round earth, and finding there
A refuge and a triumph.
    (*To* MADAME ROLAND.) Fare thee well,
Fair priestess of our goddess !   May'st though reign
A queen with her, or, falling, shine a star
To lead the unborn children on to fame,
When our weak dust is scattered !   Fare thee well !
            [*Exit* BARBAROUX, *singing as he goes.*

        If hope here fails, our Southern vales
            Shall see us firm united ;
        Come day, come night, we fall or fight
            Till Liberty be righted.

        A solemn band, with life in hand,
            To give or keep all ready,
        We firmly bare our swords, and dare
            Our foe, with voices steady.

C

Where'er we roam we'll make our home
A terror to the tyrant ;
Then traitor, fear, but hold us dear,
Blest Liberty's aspirant.

[*His voice dies away in the distance.* ROLAND
*continues to gaze fixedly at the marked maps,
then commences to write.* MADAME ROLAND.
*with clasped hands, dreamily soliloquises.*

### MADAME ROLAND.

How strange it seems that we, who so much need
Forgiveness for our actions, should hold back
Our pardon for a weakness in a friend,
And put our base constructions on those deeds
We cannot understand, being not him,
But outside all his feelings and his soul :
How can we know the workings of his heart?
The weak spot here, the tender feeling there,
The influence of a word, a look, a sigh—
The hardness of a scar which once has bled
Until it lost all feeling !   Even Louis
Has rights on his side, and should not be hurled
From off his tottering throne, could we but see
A chance of justice for our citizens
Beneath its shadow.   Ah ! the upas-tree
Is this vile Catholic Church, who ever strives
To crush all actions and all aims beyond
Her own too-narrow doors!   Could we but free
Our country from the altar and the throne,
Then Liberty might blossom ; but I fear
This shedding blood to water her dry roots
Will never make her flourish.

(*She pauses.*)                    Am I right
(The doubt will come, when lonely with my soul
I commune) in thus seeking to cast down
These long-established landmarks? Do I serve
The God I worship, when I overturn
The altar, and cast forth the canting priest
To howl his curses in a foreign land?
And am I really anxious to set up
Sublime religion of humanity
Upon the broken columns of the Church ;
And plant the holy tree of Liberty
Upon the ruins of an earthly throne?
I trust I am, but still this haunting doubt
Will backward rush, if I am quite sincere,
Or if in cobwebbed corner of my mind
There dwells some decked-out image of myself
In Liberty's blest semblance : can it be
That under all professions of high aims,
And noble thoughts, there lurks that grinning shame
Of egotism? that poison of the mind !
Oh God, alone Thou knowest my inmost soul,
If it be pure, as Thou would'st have it pure ;
If not, oh tear the veil away from me,
And let all people see the sham I am,
That having no retreat, I straight may flee
Unto Thy feet, and weeping there may learn
To make my life and words at one with Thine !

## Scene VIII.

*Little* Marie *rushes in, all flushed with running, flowers in her hands, and red Phrygian cap upon her head.*

### MADAME ROLAND.

Come my best loved one, come my little one,
Come kiss thy mother's lips and charm away
The dark thoughts which perplex her ; come and tell
Me where my pet has been, and what she saw.

                              *[Notices the red cap.*

What hast thou on thy head, oh daughter mine?
Too young and innocent art thou to don
That sign of bloody madness.   Come to me.

       *[Takes the child in her arms, and throws down the*
       *cap.*

### MARIE.

Ah mother, take these flowers ! for thee, for thee,
I gathered them this morning; but oh! see
They're sprinkled with red drops, and when I shrank
Away from them in fear, a great man said—
(A great man with red hair and starting eyes,
Who frightened me, and made me cry for thee),
'Take them, oh child, 'tis dew of liberty!
Go, take them to thy mother, and bid her
Weave thee a chaplet for la guillotine.'
What meant he, mother? 'tis not pretty dew
Like we had long ago on our white flowers,
So sparkling in the sunbeams, and so clear;

I like not Paris dew.  I took the flowers
Because a woman kissed me soft, and smiled
To the big man, and whispered : ' Baby hands
Were never meant for blood,' and placed this cap
Upon my head with, ' Bless thee, little lamb !'

MADAME ROLAND.

Bless thee, my little lamb!                    [*Kissing her.*
                        Give me the flowers,
Fair Liberty has no such dew as this ;
No blood is on her flowers, but precious dew
Falls heaven-like from heaven, and makes them free
From this pollution.  Kiss thy father, love,
And then to dreamland, where thy little soul
May roam amidst the angels' dewy flowers.
        [MARIE *kisses* ROLAND, *who is still immersed in*
        *study, then runs back to her mother coaxingly.*

MARIE.

Marie is good, and wants mamma's sweet song.

MADAME ROLAND.

Poor little darling!  I had quite forgot ;
Marie shall have the song, and then to sleep.

(*Sings.*)

Lily-buds folded
    Whisper ' good-night ;'
Roses dew-laden
    Turn from the light ;
Stars in their brightness
    Gem the deep skies :
Close now, my darling,
    Thy tirèd eyes.

Angels are weaving
　Dreams for thy soul,
While their star-chariots
　Round the sun roll—
Dream, till their star-eyes close,
Wake not till sunlight glows.

We must be working
　While thou may'st sleep,
And o'er thy young heart
　Angels watch keep ;
May all love bless thee,
　Keep thee from harm,
And God's peace hold thee
　Safe from alarm !
God's love down-shower
　Lily-heart mild,
Rose-love and beauty
　On my own child !
Rest till the morning breaks,
Sleep till the bird awakes.

[*The little one's eyes gradually close, and as*
MADAME ROLAND *very softly sings the last
notes she has fallen asleep.* MADAME ROLAND
*takes her in her arms and exit.*

# ACT II.

## SCENE I.—*In the Street.*

THÉROIGNE DE MÉRICOURT, S. HURUGE, ROSSIG-
NOL, JOURDAIN, *&c. &c., afterwards* RAOUL.

THÉROIGNE *in a riding habit the colour of blood,
a plume of the same hue upon her helmet, her
dark hair streaming below it, grasping in her
hand the sabre voted to her at the taking of the
Bastille, rides across the scene, followed in a few
moments by crowds of men, women, and children
and the above mentioned, all shouting and singing scraps of ' Ça ira,' ' Carmagnole,' and other
revolutionary songs.*

### THÉROIGNE

*(riding across the scene alone, brandishing her sabre).*

To arms !  To arms !  This is the day at last
In which my hatred of the race shall find
A breast to strike at, and that breast a queen's ;
A queen forsooth ! a queen like unto me,
Whom all men scoff at, while they bow the knee !
Just such a queen, no more ; yet she shall feel
The sharpness and the anguish of this sword
Piercing her heart, and thro' her heart the king's.
Ah, how I hate these men ! the fickle worms !

Now shouting ' Long-live Louis !' and now, ' Death
Unto the traitor !'   Do they call me mad?
'Tis such a madness as they gave to me
Thro' outraged love, thro' hope's death, and thro'
    hell!                  [*People appear on the scene.*

THÉROIGNE (*aloud to* S. HURUGE).

And you are mad, they say, and I am mad.
Well, let our madness make itself a way
Where sanity would pause.   Let's to the king :
Deeds we can do (our madness for a cloak)
Will make the sane world tremble in its path,
And all the blinking stars shut up their eyes
In horror at our madness.
          (*To the People, raising her voice.*)
                    Are you sure
You know the project thoroughly?   To-day
We need each one, and each one must be armed
Not only with a sword, but with firm will
To cast all pity for the trait'rous brood
Away from patriot heart, and be resolved
To die perchance, at any rate to kill.

PEOPLE *shout wildly*

                    We are resolved,
Lead us but on, we'll die but never pity!
(*Renewed shouting of*)   Liberty, Fraternity, Equality !
Death!   Death!   Death!

S. HURUGE (*leading the shout*).

               Death!   Death !   Death !
That is our watchword ; let it sound to-day

In triumph o'er the ruins of that place
The tyrant has polluted.   On, my friends !
I (once a noble) cast from me the name
With loathing and with horror !   I am mad,
Yea drunk with nobles' treasons, and will strike
Each noble thro' the heart, were he my son.
Ah ! would the whole accursèd race were sons
That I might quick destroy them !   Liberty,
Equality, Fraternity are now
But names, tho' loud ye shout them ; but to-day
Shall prove their strength, and make them truths
     indeed.                    [*Renewed shouting.*

THÉROIGNE (*hurriedly to* JOURDAIN).

Ha ! look you there, my God ! who is that man
Creeping and shrinking with a traitor's gait ?
Some dastard noble, spying for the king.
Drag him up here, and let the people taste
Their christening cup of vengeance.
     [JOURDAIN *rushes forward, seizes and drags the
     disguised* RAOUL *before* THÉROIGNE.

JOURDAIN.
                              Here he is ;
The man your vulture eye sought out to pledge
The people in a sacramental blood
As strengthening for the combat : look at him
And gloat o'er all his terrors, ere you pierce
His traitor heart.
     [RAOUL *stands for a moment motionless, stupefied,
     gazing at* THÉROIGNE, *then throws himself at
     her feet, catches her habit, and speaks quickly in
     a low voice.*

RAOUL.

Can you forget the time,
The happy time long past, when you and I
Thought but of love, and wished no other thought?
When innocent and sweet, you roamed the fields,
Made sweeter by your passing; when the stars
Seemed but to shine that we might be at rest
And dream each of the other; when the morn
Brought life and gladness, and the twitt'ring bird
Sang at your lattice 'Love! love! love!' alone,
And you were satisfied?   Have you forgot?
It cannot be, you must remember now!
How can you, with the sweet thought of our love,
Pour out my blood, that this loud rav'ning mob
May crush the lips you kissed, and set its heel
Upon this heart where you once loved to rest?
You must remember—save me! save me now!

THÉROIGNE (*passionately*).

Do I remember?   God! could I forget?
And happy would'st thou be could I forget,
And all my world I'd give, could I forget!
But shame is burned into my brow with fire,
And Cain-brand never dies: yet thou shalt feel
If not th' eternal anguish that I know,
Yet some faint likeness.   If reproach could kill
Eternally, it should; if by a word,
One little word, the simplest 'yea,' or 'nay,'
I could restore thee to thy home and friends,
And better actions in the time to come,
And sweeter hopes of heaven by human love

(Not passion as was ours), my tongue should cleave
Unto my mouth, and straight be torn from thence
Ere I would speak it!   Canst thou come to me,
To me, to whom the wide world is a hell,
More wretched far than hells that bigots frame ;
To me, whose simple joy in light, and air,
Bright flowers, blue skies, bird-songs, and lover's
    voice,
And innocent home pleasures, was so great,
Until thou cam'st and cursed me?   Is it sin
Thus to revenge my father's, mother's, sighs,
Dying grief-stricken on their lowly hearth ;
My brothers', sisters', shame, that I was shamed;
Joy crushed from out our lives, and that sad soul
In me, for which Christ died, hustled away
From heaven's gate ; that thou perchance might feel
One moment all the wild beast in thee glad
And passion have her way?   Have I forgot?
                    [*Laughing wildly*
Judge now ; look in my eyes ; have I forgot?

### RAOUL.

Ah Théroigne, I wronged you !   Pardon me,
As you may hope for pardon in God's love.

### THÉROIGNE.

'God's love' !   you've made me doubt it if it be ;
And even if it be round-clasping earth,
And over-shadowing mountains with its wings,
It cannot shelter me.   Have I not sinned
Beyond forgiveness?   Father's, mother's curse
Would drag me from before the golden throne,

God's presence-seat, if angels bore me there !
Talk not of love to me, pardon to me,
Whose life is one long vengeance.  I shall fall
By these same tigers I now gorge with blood,
Revenge thus ever back rebounds—I know
It cannot last for ever ; but by heaven
Thou shalt not see my fall ! and in that hell
Thou'st made for me, thy spirit shall be first
To greet mine on its entrance.

RAOUL.

       There's no hope ?  .   .   .
I can but die then.   Be it as you will :
The time may come when you will have out-grown
This childish thirst for vengeance ; as it is
You are not great enough—not high enough
To pardon: I have sinned to God and you,
I know and do confess it ; you can kill
My body and take vengeance on my flesh,
But for my soul I have it in His care ;
And if that hell you rave of be as deep
As your revenge, He yet can rescue me,
And make a ladder of His punishments
For my soiled soul to climb by.   Strike me now !
    [THÉROIGNE *hesitates;* ROSSIGNOL, *coming for-*
    *ward scoffingly.*

ROSSIGNOL.

What ! our fair Liégoise struck dumb by him !
Where is her courage ?   Where ? Is he her love,
This milk-faced traitor ?   That he did her wrong
Seems now his boast ; no doubt his heaven's pledge :

God is no sans-culotte, and noble's joys
Must be provided, let who suffer may :
The ewe-lamb of the people must be slain
And garnished gaily for the noble's feast,
While God looks on, and angels deck the board :
We want no noble's god !   Strike down the man,
And let his blood a morning offering be
To freedom, brothers !   Strike him !   down with him !
    [*A hundred knives are pushed forward.*  RAOUL
    *falls lifeless in a pool of blood;* THÉROIGNE
    *watches him fall, and then turns to* ROSSIGNOL.

THÉROIGNE.

Am I struck dumb by him?   This day will show !
Come, pledge me in his blood !
    [*She dips her hand into the pool of blood and touches
    it with her lips.*

                              Such was my hate
For him, my Judas, could I sip each drop
'Twould be to me as nectar, did he feel
The anguish of a death drawn slowly out ;
I'd give my soul to torment thro' all time
To gain it him, were Paradise for me
With him to share it !   Now I'm mad indeed ;
Let us not talk, his blood has made me fierce
For Louis' blood.
    [*She gallops on, followed by the crowd.*

SCENE II.—*The* Tuileries, *a room opening out of another.*

LOUIS (*alone*).

Alas ! alas ! life seems some baleful dream !
I feel this nightmare of the mind must end
Or life shall cease for me ; I cannot live
Thus ; ever thinking when the sun dawns fair
' To-day will be the last : '—and yet it goes
(Ah God, how slowly !) and the anguished hours
Drag themselves on, and still I live, and still
I suffer, as none suffered, sure, before.
What have I done ?   What direful sin in me
Calls down such vengeance on my erring heart ?
I know not, and my holy Catholic Church
Finds no fault in me.   Show me, oh my God !
Where is my crime, that I may cast it out,
And save my queen and children from this hour,
This ever-growing hour of shame and woe.—
Was I not born a king ? and now they say
(These rabble sans-culottes) because my sire
Bequeathed to me a crown, it is my sin
That I have worn it in the time gone by
As 'twere not their good gift ; their gift, forsooth !
What can they know of God-anointed kings
Heaven sends to curb their humours, and keep down
This base-born rabble in its native mud—
God sends them to obey, and us to reign ;
They envy what's beyond them ; could they teach
Me all their meanness and coarse thoughts, and oaths,
Then might I reign in peace, the nation's king,

As Roland is its minister.  'Fore God,
Rather than yield one inch of royal grace,
I'll shed my royal blood ! and they shall see
Their tortures have not tamed me, while their crime
Shall bring them vengeance from all kings on earth,
And the Great King in heav'n, who sent me here,
Me, His anointed, to defend His church. . . .
And yet, my wife, my children—what for you
Remains were I to fall ? can I not save
You from these traitors ?  I would glad submit
For your dear sakes—if need be, I must feign
Submission for the time—would I were dead,
Ere, shamed and scoffed at by my father's slaves,
I, Louis, stoop to falsehood !  And God knows
I've ever borne this people in my heart,
And sought their good, if not their liberties :
Could I have giv'n them bread, how willingly
Should corn have ripened o'er the land's wide plain,
And hunger never seeded to revolt ;
'Twas not my fault ; I never took their food,
Or burned their houses, or laid waste their fields,
Or tore their daughters from their cottage homes
To my embraces ; no ; I never wronged
One man of all the nation, and yet now
They seek my death, with outcries fierce for blood
Of all my house, more innocent than I.

> [*He sighs deeply, rests his head on his hands and
> appears sunk in thought, and quite oblivious of
> the shouts and curses which have begun to echo
> round the palace, as the crowd, led by* S. HURUGE,
> THÉROIGNE, *etc., march up and surround it,
> pouring in at every opening ; at length they begin*

*to batter the door with cries of* 'Where is the
Tyrant?' 'Show us the Austrian Woman !'

LOUIS (*starting up to two lackeys who wait in the
adjoining room*).

Throw the doors open ; let the rabble see
I fear them not ; throw the doors open wide !

---

## SCENE III.

*He folds his arms, and advances to the excited
mob as the doors are thrown open.*

#### LOUIS.

You called for me, my people ? here I am !
Behold me, Louis, King of France and you !
The doors are open, enter then and see
Your monarch and your father.

#### JOURDAIN (*furiously*).

                    Fear you not?
A hundred swords are thirsting for your blood ;
A hundred knives are trembling in the hands
Of your would-be assassins.

#### LOUIS (*calmly*).

                    Fear ?   Why fear?
I feel no fear ; what cause have I to fear
While standing 'midst my people ?   Here I am,

Your king:—the hundred swords may drink my blood,
And then? why then they in their turn drink yours
For leading them to mine.—I fear you not.

> [*People shout* 'Down with the Veto!' THÉ-
> ROIGNE *rushes in, pressed forward by the crowd
> surging on.*

THÉROIGNE.

Where is the traitor Louis? Let my sword
(Won on the Bastille, where his tyrant will
Did patriot hearts to death, and where the tree
Of Liberty now blooms), let my sword pierce
His coward heart, and hers, and all the brood.
Oh Jezebel of France, thine hour is come!
Thy blood shall be poured out before all men,
And this thine Ahab, led to crime by thee,
Be witness, and be sharer in thy shame.

LOUIS (*confronting her*).

What have I done to thee, that thou dost thirst
To sheathe thy sword in innocent pure hearts
Of women and of children? Let me learn
The crime which drives thee, young and fair thyself.
In madness to cast down thy sex and age
And league thyself with murder. Drop thy sword.
Oh woman! those white fingers should be kissed
By lover's warm lips, not by sword's cold steel;
Thy wondrous beauty should fill hearts with joy,
Not lash them into madness.

THÉROIGNE.

           Drop my sword!
I'll cling to it, the one thing left to me,

Till death takes both !—Thou art a traitor, thou—
Seek not with soft fair words to turn my wrath
(My wrath against mankind) from thy false breast,
I strike for Liberty !   For vengeance !—

> [*Strikes out furiously; one of the officers who have
> now joined the king pushes up her arm, and she
> is forced back by the advancing crowd.*

ROSSIGNOL (*handing up a Phrygian cap on the top of a
pike*).

If thou indeed art king, and lovest us,
Put on the people's colours ; crown thyself
With Liberty's insignia.

> [LOUIS *takes the cap and places it on his head;
> shouts of* ' Long live the king !' *immediately re-
> sound through the room.*

LOUIS.

Oh my friends !
Did you but know my heart, you soon would see
Your colours there ; your wishes graven there !

> [*Cries from below in the gardens,* 'Strike down
> the tyrant !' 'Throw down his head!' *etc.   A
> beggar passes up a bottle.*

BEGGAR.

An Louis loves us, let him drink to us.

LOUIS (*takes the bottle and drinks fearlessly*).

I drink the people's health, and may they learn
How dear and precious to their patriot king
Is their good health and comfort.—Your good health !

> [*Renewed shouts of* ' Long live King Louis the

people's king !' *The crowd opens, and makes way*
*respectfully for* PÉTION *with escort of* National
Guards.  PÉTION *hastening to the king's side.*

---

## SCENE IV.

### PÉTION.

I trust, Sire, you are safe ; I but now heard
Of this tumultuous greeting, and came fast
To bid your lieges  .  .  .  .

LOUIS (*haughtily interrupting him*).

Peace ! I want no words
To speak your service ; words are more than vain
When actions contradict them.—Do your will,
But prate not of your loyalty to me.

[*Turns away.*

PÉTION (*addressing the mob who begin to retire, and*
*make way for him*).

I, Pétion, do request you for the law
Disperse, and to your homes ; the time goes fast,
And evening shades draw on ; return then now :
Your mission is accomplished, and the king
Has personally heard, and strongly pledged
Himself to your petition.   Citizens,
I pray you leave the palace and return
As you did come, for Liberty and law ;
Not for revenge, or personal small aims,
But with all moderation, to make clear

Your wishes to the king : those wishes heard,
Disperse, ere it be said your patriot aim
Was not for Liberty, and right and truth,
But for sedition, pillage, robbery—
I, Pétion, do request you to disperse
In the name of law, and your assembly.

> [*Cries of* ' Long live PÉTION !' ' Hurrah for Law
> and Liberty !' *People gradually disperse.*

---

### SCENE V.

PÉTION *and* LOUIS.

PÉTION.

You now are free, Sire ; what are your commands?

LOUIS (*bitterly*).

'Twas not your fault I am not free indeed,
Free from the life your friends have made a curse.
Commands?   I take them—I have none to give—
My one command is (and that one a prayer
Since I cannot enforce it), leave me now,
If possible, in peace.

PÉTION.

Sire, I am gone.

> [*Exeunt* PÉTION *and* National Guards.

LOUIS (*alone*).

Where is the queen?   I trust that I alone
Was favoured by this greeting, ' for the law '—

The law of base desires, the devil's law,
To judge it by its fruits.—I'll to the queen.
                    [*Exit* LOUIS.

---

## SCENE VI.

*The* Queen *in a bow window, a heavy table rolled in front of her for protection, on which is seated the* Dauphin *with the Phrygian cap on his head, the* Princess *leaning close against the* Queen *who has her arm round her. Everything in disorder, tables and chairs overturned—carpets torn up, pictures scattered over the floor—the* Queen *striving to appear calm but with tears in her eyes.* PRINCESS de LAM-BALLE *returning from looking out of the door.*

PRINCESS DE LAMBALLE.

They've gone at last, my queen ; the last foul face
Has passed your royal doors ; and now in peace
You can repose and weep.
            [MARIE ANTOINETTE *comes from behind the table
            and throws herself into an armchair.*
                    My queen !  My queen !
                    (*Passionately weeping*).
Ah ! could I bear this shame and agony,
So that thy royal head might ne'er be bowed,
How willingly I would !  My queen ! my queen !
Would that my love for thee a shield might be
To quench their hatred, and beat back their scorn !
Oh could this breast receive blows aimed at thee,
'Twould count them kisses. Oh my queen ! my queen !
            [*She throws her arms round her and kisses her.*

## SCENE VII.

*Enter* LOUIS, *the Phrygian cap still on his head; the* Queen *rises and* LOUIS *receives her in his arms; the* Children *press close to them.*

LOUIS.

Ah Madame, you are safe then !   God be praised !
But why this desolation?   Did they come
(This rebel people) with threats for your ears
And trait'rous cries?   My God !   Why did I bring
You from your fatherland to share my crown !
A crown of misery—had I but known  .  .  .  .

*[Stops overcome.*

MARIE ANTOINETTE *(tenderly).*

Dear Louis, speak not thus :  I would not change
Our danger if I could, so it be ' ours,'
Not ' mine,' or ' thine,' but ' ours :'—we are alone
When 'mine' or 'thine' comes first, but 'ours' sounds
        sweet
E'en now—the bitter-sweet they've left to us.
        *(Sees the Phrygian cap upon his head.)*
Oh Louis, cleanse thy brow from that foul sign,
The image of revolt, of treason, death—
And worse than death, dishonour—tear it off
And trample it.—Ah heaven !  on my child
I see its sign of blood.

*[Tears it off the* Dauphin's *head, and tramples it underfoot.*

                Can I forget
The poisoned words of him who placed it there?

Words I can ne'er repeat, and ne'er forgive,
They're branded on my soul !   That I, a queen,
A woman, should be forced by coward slaves
And rebels such as these, to hear my name
Made filthy by their lips—marred by their thoughts—
And dragged thro' deeds I dreamed not of !   A wife
Abused by that dear name (most tender, sweet,
And holy of all names), which I have striven,
As best I knew, to keep as lily-pure
As when it first was mine—a child reviled
Because of her proud lineage !   Oh my friend,
Unutterable words I've heard to-day,
An Austrian, a wife, can ne'er forgive !
My heart is sore with bearing—I must rest,
Or weak flesh will betray me ; I shall quail
Beneath the hating eyes which hunt me down
And count each hard-wrung tear a triumph pearl
To deck their envy with : poor triumph, theirs—
To force the Austrian's tears from her sad eyes
For country lost—love lost—all lost—would life
Were lost with all the rest !—Farewell to you ;
Yield not one step ; we all must die at last,
'Twill be but sooner.—Struggle to the end !

       [*Exeunt* Queen, Children, *and* LAMBALLE.

---

## SCENE VIII.

### LOUIS (*alone*).

Why did I bring her from her happy home
So lovely and so proud ? I can recall

When first a bride she flashed thro' all the land
'Mid glimmering jewels, drums, and triumph shouts—
All people loving her for her fair face
And gracious words—a blessing and a crown
To this gay land, and me ; and now to-day,
Instead of those blithe shouts, and merry jests,
A cursing from all mouths, and swords upraised
To pierce our helpless bosoms.  Ah my God,
' Thy ways are not our ways ' !   I cannot tell
If this be sent me for my sins gone-by,
Or crimes of my fore-fathers (*pauses*).   It is past
For this once more ; the death-wave has rolled back,
And left us stranded ; but another tide
Will bear us from all landmarks far away
Into the surging ocean of revolt,
Which knows no bounds or fetters but—a grave.

    [*Covers his face with his clasped hands and leans
       forward on the table overcome with sadness.*

# ACT III.

## SCENE I.

*A Wood near Paris, sunlight and shadow amidst the trees.* BARBAROUX *and* CAMILLE DESMOULINS *walking.*

### BARBAROUX.

How lovely Nature seems after the din
Of rival factions ! how her beauty falls,
Like dew in summer, on our weary hearts
Made thirsty, and worn sore by constant strain,
In clanging Paris ! Almost I could cast
The crown of fame I strive for to the winds,
And grasp the poet's crown of fresh green leaves
I feel within my reach. We are not one,
Friend, in our aims, but in our poets' joy
We are united, and fair Nature's voice
Speaks to our hearts alike, and speaks to-day.

### CAMILLE.

What ! Barbaroux, my firebrand of the South !
Is that thy voice, which speaks of poets' joys,
Despising heroes' ? Can it be indeed
The daring man who summoned from Marseilles
The Revolution's spirit and its song ?

BARBAROUX.

' How well and wisely spake the Christ of old
" Ye cannot serve two masters ; " that will hold
While the world lasts ; if love we choose to serve
We must resign all else, and strain each nerve
To do her bidding ; but if we aspire
To Godlike intellect, that divine fire
Crowning the grand art-heights, and hope to reach
The summit of all glory, we must teach
Our hearts to beat responsive to no touch
Of earth, or earth's allurements, we must clutch
Our nature, nor release, till pale and dead
It takes each hue of art, and passive led
Drags no more backward to the joys behind
Whose voices faintly reach us down the wind
As upward still we climb, and never rest
(Or dream of resting) on a dearer breast
Than earth's, which greets us coldly at the last
When art is realised, for life is past ! '
So wrote a poet once ; he felt its truth
As I feel it to-day ; and yet I know
I still shall join the combat, and shall strive
As I have striven before.—Ah Camille ! thou
Canst understand this weakness, and dost know
Our actions seldom show the best in us,
But only passion's strength in mastery :
What's loveliest is weakest in our souls.

CAMILLE.

Dear friend, I catch your meaning, and I know
Your actions noble as the heart which prompts,

Though I, a poet, feel my poet's soul
All glorious in the combat for our rights ;
I triumph in the battle, and could shout
My song of triumph as the traitors fall
And Liberty blooms free !   No vain regrets
Hold back my hand from grasping the sharp sword
And piercing traitor hearts.   I feel inspired
To fight and sing together, as they fall ;
But there are voiceless poets, whose deep souls
Can ne'er express one half the mystery
They find in their own depths, so silently
Make their life sing, what words are weak to say ;
The greatest are like this, and you are one ;
But your life speaks, a glorious burning speech,
A hymn of Liberty, which we can hear,
And carry in our hearts, and combat for !

### BARBAROUX.

Your words describe not me, but speak of her,
Our voice, our inspiration ! at whose side
Cowards grow brave, and traitors become true ;
Our own fair Roland, noblest, truest, best
Of all her sex ; the strongest and most free,
The emblem of our faith—of Liberty !

### CAMILLE.

The thought of her inspires us, each and all,
To combat to the end, with voice, and sword,
And life, and deed—her presence goes before
Like fiery cloud, and leads us ever on,
Nor hell nor devil bar our victory.

[*They turn towards Paris.*

## BARBAROUX.

This silence is not healthy ; I misgive
This most unusual silence ; these last weeks
Our Paris has scarce breathed ; 'twill prove, I trust,
The calm before the thunder, cleansing quick
With mighty force the creeping pestilence,
Then passing into peace ; not the fierce storm
Which sweeps o'er earth destroying, nor takes count
Of its own ravage, seeking but to slay.

## CAMILLE.

This Paris, once let loose, will rage, I fear,
With boundless ruin : throne and altar down,
It will attack its leaders ;—but who fears ?
We shall at least have triumphed, and the end
We have no power to see, and no desire.
We struggle to surmount the jaggèd cliff
Of popular favour, that most giddy height,
Yet still surmountable to clinging hands,
And hearts resolved to conquer ; but beware !
Look not behind, the precipice below
Will chill thy courage, paralyse thy strength,
And cast thee shuddering down the dread abyss
Passed safely if not thought of : tremble not,
Who trembles falls—but who with stedfast eye
Looks up unshrinking, he shall reach the heights,
And victory shall crown him at the top !—
The present is my god : I would be free
From king and church, that won—then—then—why
    then—
We'll think what more to strive for.

[*They enter Paris.*

See, my friend,
Our sleeping breathless Paris hath awaked
From her short slumber ; hear the cries and shouts !
Some deed is doing I were loth to lose.
Come, let us hasten.   ˙            [*They pass on rapidly.*

---

## SCENE  II.

*A  Street  in  Paris ;  crowd  appear  bearing  a  bullock's
heart  pierced,  with  the  inscription  'Aristocrat's
heart.'   People  shouting* 'Down  with  the  tyrant !'
'Long live* ROLAND !' 'ROBESPIERRE, the people's
friend, for ever ! '

### CAMILLE.

Who shouts for Roland and Robespierre ?
I shout with you, but wherefore shout to-day ?

### 1ST CITIZEN.

Where have you come from, that you do not know ?

### 2ND CITIZEN.

You must be traitor since you do not know.

### 3RD CITIZEN.

His face speaks treason, strike the traitor down !

### CAMILLE (*drawing his sword*).

What, citizens !   I, Camille, I your friend,
And you not know me ?   Shame upon your eyes,

So blinded, you forget your faithful friends !
Shame on you, shame ! Throw down your swords, or I
Will hew them from your hands.

### 1ST CITIZEN.

It is a friend.

### 2ND CITIZEN.

Why ! our brave Camille, here's long life to thee,
Our patriot poet ! If our eyes were dim,
'Twas blindness from the traitor.

*[Crowd passes on with renewed shouting.*

---

### SCENE III.

ROLAND's *House, interior.* ROLAND, MADAME ROLAND.

### ROLAND.

     I still fear
This Paris must be left, and in the South
Our withered Liberty take root again ;
The people sleep, and in their dreamless rest
Seem to forget that slumber must mean death
To those on precipice of tyrant's faith :—
' Down with the Veto ! ' has now died away
Into grim silence, and the tyrant's star
Seems brightening in its course for the eclipse
It suffered with that cry. Could we unite,
We well might dare the world, with all its kings,
Its armies, and its pride, to cast us down,
But as it is, I tremble. Robespierre

Keeps his ideas so secret, friend or foe
Ne'er know his object ; when his speech seems fair
'Tis but to mask its depth.

MADAME ROLAND.

Fear not, my friend,
He is with us, I feel it ; did we not
Save him when threatened ? how then could he cast
Suspicion over us ?   His only fault
Is that one weakness, he is true as steel
To Liberty and us—but hear those shouts,
They sound not like deep slumber ; 'tis thy name
I hear them shout, and his, in concert too,
A happy omen.

SCENE IV.

*People appear under the windows, shouting*
' Long live ROLAND and ROBESPIERRE ! '
' Hurrah for DANTON ! '   ' Liberty, Equality,
Fraternity ! '   ' Down with all tyrants ! '   BUZOT
*rushes in hurriedly.*

BUZOT.

Roland, they shout for you ;
The patriot ministry is back recalled—
The people joy—all parties are at one—
Show thyself now ; the tyrant is deposed
And lodged within the Temple ! show thyself.

[ROLAND *goes to the window.   Renewed shouting
as before.*

Thanks, friends and citizens ! you make me proud
To hear my humble name resounding clear
With sacred Liberty's : I firmly trust
They e'er may be united,—that my deeds
Be lighted ever by those triple lamps
I bear within my heart.      [*Great shouting.*
            Yet, one more word :
I would beseech you conquering people,
As ye have triumphed, be ye merciful
In your great triumph ; let it ne'er be said
The sons of Liberty forgot their queen,
And trampled on the banner they had raised ;
Shed not your brothers' blood ; be merciful,
And raise those brothers, erring in the dark,
Not crush them in their darkness ; brothers still,
Brothers in blood and heart, they are to you.
Oh let that blessèd light shine in their eyes,
The light ye joy in, in their darkened eyes,
That they may clearly see ; and never hurl
(Because they're blinded) deeper gloom on them.
I pray you now, dear friends, be pitiful !
If ye can trust my words—be pitiful !
If I have served you well—be pitiful !
In Liberty's blest name—be pitiful !
'Tis the one lesson I would fain teach you,
Who gloriously can combat, who can die,
Nor murmur nor shrink back, can give your blood,
Your sons, your land, your all, for Liberty—
Oh Roman people, struggling for your rights,
And conquering as ye must, be pitiful !

'Tis my last word, your service calls me now :
Farewell brave citizens, be pitiful !

[ROLAND *bows and retires. People continue shouting, then gradually retire.*

---

## SCENE V.

ROLAND *coming back from the window. Enter* DANTON,
ROBESPIERRE, BRISSOT, &c.  MADAME ROLAND,
BUZOT *as before.*

### DANTON.

Roland, you've heard the news?  United now
All parties march together—on—on—on—
Till naught remains to conquer, none to die !
No power can curb us, no power but our wills.
Hurrah for our Republic ! let the name
Be shouted till the echo, speaking it,
Gives forth no other tone—until each tongue
Grows weary with the utt'rance and forgets
All other forms of speech—until the names
King, monarchy, and treason, have no sense,
And yield no meaning to the intellect :
Hurrah for our Republic ! now at last
I can breathe openly ; all other thoughts
Of Louis' fate, the war, our private aims,
Can be deferred : triumphantly we'll shout
That magic name Republic ! far and wide
Its glory shall be seen, we'll swift convert
The whole dull world to our great Liberty !
What matter thousands falling ? their red blood

E

Will make the plains more fertile, and send up
A stronger, greener, tree of Liberty.
Mow down the fruitless ears, and clear the grain
From useless growing weeds, which suck the fields
Dry, for their uselessness, and leave the corn
All with'ring in the sun-glare—mow them down ;
Let no false pity for the sickly things
Urge us to spare them :—mow them swiftly down,
And clear a path across their fallen stems
For our Republic's passage.

MADAME ROLAND.

                    Nay, my friend ;
Our blessèd new Republic scarce will pass
With tender feet across such bloody paths :
How would her beauteous face be marred and wan,
Her glory crushed away, and that pure brow
Star-crowned, be lowered, low as human hearts,
When they can stoop to vengeance !   To forgive,
To pity, pardon—should be her high aims,
Not to cut down the erring ; will the world
Receive as goddess, she, who ruthlessly
Tears up the strong roots of her smiling flowers,
Useless perhaps, in contrast with the corn,
And yet to those whose souls can pierce below
The shell of things, and note the mind beneath,
More useful than the grain—that can but feed
This human nature, this poor body's lust,
Which perishes so soon ; but they lift up
The spirit of our souls, and heaven-high
Raise our weak nature (not but nourish it
At present height), and by their beauty-crown
Mingle the usual in the infinite.

ROBESPIERRE.

To talk in poetry is doubtless good ;
But to my mind the abstract should be sunk
Into the depths of present need and act.
'Tis not what we would wish, or love, or gain,
Or what in pure philosophy should live ;
Or what ideal republics might be made ;
But what the people need, what we can do
For their deliv'rance ;—not what should be done
By raising human nature to the stars,
But what our present nature leaves to us,
That seems to me the question ; we are men,
                    [*Turning to* MADAME ROLAND.
And you speak only from your woman heart
In urging us to pity.  I am one
Who turn most woman-like from sight of blood,
And shrink to doom e'en traitors unto death.
But 'tis not question now of 'like' or 'leave,'
The vermin in our path must be crushed down,
Or they will turn and rend us.  No man's death
Or woman's sorrow shall be due to us
Unless from strict necessity, to clear
The path for our Republic ; then indeed
Tremble the traitors who would stay our course !
We'll mow them down by thousands, yea the earth
Shall be once more a void, before we pause.

BRISSOT.

You speak, Robespierre, as you ever spoke,
A patriot clear and true ; no other thought
Dwells in your mind but Liberty ; we know

E 2

How faithful you have been, and still will be :
For traitors in our path, let them beware,
We'll hurl them from us swiftly ; but I hold
We're strong enough to pardon, and to wait
Till slow conviction drives the mist away
From brothers' hearts, and lets in that clear light
Which glads our own.

ROLAND.

My own opinion
But now given to the people ; mercy yet
Is only justice ; let the present show
Our new Republic's beauty ;—soon these men
Who horror-struck recoil, will swift return
And join us, brothers in the victory.
The battle is half won, now we again
Stand firm united, and with close-clasped hands
And eyes straight gazing into brother-eyes
Together grasp the problem ; we are strong
In all that makes men strong, firm faith and trust
In our Republic, courage to cast down
Our present good for future weal of her ;
Then being strong, let us be merciful ;
Not merciful as fools are merciful,
Who spare the serpent coiling round their throats,
Or merciful as cowards, who refrain
From casting from them traitors, lest they turn
And randomly strike home ; no : merciful
As Romans knew of mercy, ere the lust
Of blood (which grows in shedding) filled their hearts
And choked out reason's voice, and so they fell.

BUZOT.

Oh Roman Roland, wisely dost thou speak !
My voice with thine for mercy, while we dare
Together banded, scoff at threats and woes :
Our dawning life in future shall not be
The conqueror's lust of old ; no : we will prove
The greatness of our end by stooping low
And gath'ring the crushed bloom from out the dust
To crown our goddess' brows ; all nature's heart
Shall be at one with ours, we'll count her throbs
By listening to our own, her blissful throbs
When springing swift the tender violet,
And dewy gleaming lily lie revealed,
And show her thoughts ; while reveries of grass
And high dreams of fair trees, adorn the world,
And wake in poets echoes of their birth
In mighty soul of Nature :—can we not
In such wise make our thoughts, our dreams, our
        aims
Outblossom for the people? and lose count
Of pardon or of vengeance?   I misgive
This constant argument ; can we not strive
O'er-looking those who soul-straight combat us,
Not crying traitors simply, but by deeds
Swift showing them their treasons, while we still
March on, not pausing to cut down ; too great
The lion is to heed the sting of flies,
But children weary and strike out their fists
To slay the puny terror, not seeing clear
The truth of higher minds : ' Who suffers calm
Is victor, while he suffers !'   Oh my friends,

Are we not like the lion? we can bear
And live beyond this petty 'treason' cry
(The children's terror, not the lion's fear).
Is our Republic founded in our hearts
Or merely in our voices? All can shout
Her blessèd name, but time shows who can bear
Her image undefiled thro' tears and blood, .
Her white-enwrapping robe unstained, untorn,
Thro' fire of treason—murder—sacrilege.

### MADAME ROLAND.

You tell my heart-thoughts, Buzot, I can hear
In your clear voice my inmost mind expressed;
Yes, Nature is our worship, and like her
We should, with tender dew and falling rain
Of pitying sufferance to misguided hearts,
Make manifest our love; she does not choose,
Alone, the highest types to work upon
And glory by their growing; she creates
A wondrous chain of being, stretching wide
From earth's fair dawn till now, when gleaming sun,
Lighting the dimness, shows the fading forms
Of shadows, held realities in the dark :
This wondrous chain of being cast across
The mist of ages, vanishes at last
In lowest form of scarcely breathing life,
Which yet exists; while the slow-growing chain
Develops calm-browed heroes, poets crowned,
Philosophers sublime, and all the race
Holds best and noblest in the chain of life,
And, ever-lengthening while the ages roll
Their stately march, will coil thro' boundless space

Until it reach the star-heights that we see
And dream in gazing of infinity !
Our souls feel in such moments that their home
Lies far beyond the present, that its joys,
Its arguments, and questions, touch them not,
Or only brush in passing ; that they wing
Their flight (the chain completed) there to shine
As stars among the stars !  Sure 'tis enough
To wither all low motives, to believe,
And feel the surety in our inmost minds
When calmly we gaze there, that such a fate
Awaits our human nature, that each one
May help the march triumphant to the stars,
By self-development and fitness for
The crowning future. . . . But who enters now?

## Scene VI.

*Enter* Camille Desmoulins *and* Barbaroux,
*afterwards* Chamfort, *who comes in silently
and unnoticed until he speaks.* Camille *aside
to* Barbaroux *as they enter.*

### CAMILLE.

Robespierre and Danton here again !
What tempest can have wrecked them, that they
    come
To shelter calmly 'neath the Gironde's wing,
And join their voice with ours?  We now shall hear
The meaning of those patriots whe were loth

To leave my head upon its native stem,
But offered it a pike to rest upon,
Improving Nature !
(*Aloud.*)            Greet you citizens !
Is it permitted that I, too, should know
The object of your meeting, and the cause
Ot this blithe gath'ring of long sever'd friends
I joy to see once more? We've but now come
From wand'ring, dreaming, in the laughing woods,
And met a crowd of patriots who were fain
To send us seeking with their ready pikes
A path for dreams behind the gate of death,

ROBESPIERRE (*aside*).

This dreaming Gironde maunder all alike
Of dreams, and stars, and flowers.   I hate this cant !
They seek to veil behind their high-pitched shrieks
Of nature—beauty—love—their thirst for power,
The Gironde power alone, no one to share
Its shadow or its substance ;—for this time
I must dissemble, but the people soon
Will know its true friends from its dreaming ones,
Then shall these poets find their life a dream.—
(*Aloud.*)   You will regret, friend, dreaming in the
      woods,
When you hear this day's triumph ; as morn broke
The nation rose in Paris with one voice,
And surging to the Palace, forced the King
(A king no more when this speech shall be done)
To fly regardless,—massacred all those
Who rashly stood 'tween tiger and his prey,
And lodging Louis and his family

Within the Temple's hoary, time-worn walls,
Blotted the monarchy beneath a storm
Of traitor's blood for ever out of sight,
Destroyed the name of king, and leaves us now
To steel our minds to justice, on his head,
This Louis, our woe's cause : the reason this
Of all friends meeting, we have to agree
Among ourselves, his punishment, and then
In the Convention speak it.—Are you too
Minded to pity, not your own dire foe
But tyrant of the people ?  For their sake
My vote will claim his blood, and hers, and theirs,
The adulteress and her brood—they die.

MADAME ROLAND.

Oh Robespierre, blinded by thy love
Of Liberty and people, think again.
Shed not his blood, nor hers, tho' sinning, still
A helpless woman ; and the children too,
No crime have they committed ; pardon them !
If need be, let our France cast them away
From her pure bosom, in a foreign land
To wail their falsehoods and maybe repent,
At any rate regret ; oh let not us
Who preach the universal brotherhood
Inaugurate our faith with brother's blood !

BARBAROUX.

No ; exiles shall they be ; my voice I'll raise
In the Convention, and shout hoarse until
I wield them to that vote, ' exile not death !'
Death is too good for traitors, death is rest,

And peace, and sleep, and calm, no vain regrets
Or hopeless yearnings dim death's cool retreat ;—
Life is for traitors, life, and endless woe,
And sorrow ten times stronger that they know
Their own base deeds poured gall into the wine
So sweet once to their taste : ' exile not death ! '

DANTON.

If Louis were an ordinary man
One in the crowd, a traitor, still below
The glaring heights of life (on which to live
Needs marble hearts, opaque, unnoticing
Of scorching popular breath) ; if he were one
E'en in the second height of mountain scale
On which some shelter dwells, a stunted bush,
Or dwarfèd pine, or fading bramble twig
To yield some cover, e'en tho' thin and poor
To his enormities, I'd say ' forgive,'
' Exile not death,' my vote ; but as it is,
He dwelling on the topmost pinnacle,
Th' eternal peak of snow, and looking down
Upon the people worshipping below,
Did curse them as a god, and make so clear,
By contrast of that snow, his blackened soul,
That all the kneeling slaves rose up firestrung
And swept him down, and trampled ;
                    [*Pauses, then continues slowly and quietly.*
                              and were still—
That we, their chosen, might decide for them
The depth to cast him in ; earth has no gulf
So deep 'twould hide his blackness, death alone,
While blessing him with peace, not curses us

With his continual presence, maddening
Our people with his plots—his treasons—death !
For their sake I too echo, 'Louis death !'

CHAMFORT.

Methinks this close-bound brotherhood will split
Swift into fragments ; one shouts 'death ! death !
    death !'
Another cries for mercy, and exile ;
In the Convention numbers will decide,
Or eloquence may turn, but mercy's dead
I see in all our hearts—no mercy now,
And none deserved ; for my part I would rush
And drag this trembling Louis from his hole
And let the people hunt him for their sport.

ROLAND (*sadly*).

Well, the Convention must decide ; and I
Must cease to serve a nation drunk with blood,
Incapable of reason ;—if he falls
I feel the time draws near when ' Liberty'
Shall be translated ' license ;' when each one
Not for the nation, but himself, shall strike,
And hurl down power that he may build his own,
A tott'ring column on a shifting sand
Of daily popular change.

CAMILLE.

                    Night draws on ;
And prophecies dark as night grow with it.
Roland, you see but shadow, there is light
Beyond it :—were we one on each and all

The subjects for discussion, why what need
Of any words?   E'en brothers disagree
Yet love not any less that diff'rent souls
Speak from their diff'rent bodies ; we are one
In love for our Republic, and the rest
What matters it?   Good-night to all my friends.

*[Exit* CAMILLE *singing.*

Daylight swift fades away,
    Life still rolls on ;
We should be blithe and gay,
    Life still rolls on ;
Love is the light of day,
Life steals our love away ;
    Ah ! little love of mine,
    Shine thro' the darkness, shine !
        Kiss me to slumber,
            Sing me to rest,
        Sweetest my dreams are
            On thy white breast.

    Ah ! little love of mine,
        Angels above
    Know not the rapture
        Of thy sweet love ;
    Sing, little bird of mine,
        Sing silver-clear,
    Sing thro' the darkness,
        I, thy love, hear.
    Ah ! little love of mine,
    Shine thro' the darkness, shine !

*[His voice dies away in the distance.  All say good-night and exeunt.*

# ACT IV.

SCENE I.—*A Room tastefully furnished with books, pictures, etc., one of which has a silken curtain drawn over it.*

BUZOT (*alone*).

Ah God ! that she and I had met before,
    Or never met, in this world of farewells ;
Must I for ever stand without the door
    And dream and long for what my nature tells
Is mine by right of sympathy?   My soul
    Can fitly echo hers, and I express
In words her own heart-throbs ; is not our goal
    The very same?   And as I onward press
    Her soft eyes watch me with a mute caress.

I hate myself for dreaming, when to fight
    Is every Frenchman's duty ; and my arm
Is strong as ever to uphold the right
    And strike for freedom at the first alarm.
And she inspires me, yes ; my love for her
    Floats like a banner consecrating all,
Over my life ; and still I would prefer
    To combat 'neath that banner till I fall,
    So she were near me when beneath the pall

My stilled heart lay, and passionate no more
  Slept quiescent beneath her tender eyes,
Nor flushed to wilder longing as of yore,
  When she would wonder with a sweet surprise
At broken words, fire-quenched by their own might,
  Half bursting forth in passionate full speech,
And crushed (how hardly !) far out of her sight,
  Leaving but anguished eyes, whose looks beseech
  Pardon for love, her pure soul dare not reach.

I honour Liberty with soul as true
  As ever Roman bore ; and yet I know
Her image floats before me, and shines thro'
  My loftier aims, and guides me where I go ;
And thus it should be, there's no shame in this
  That seeing beauty, freedom, purity—
I love it from afar, tho' perfect bliss
  Of fond possession, and the rarity
  Of love and worship joined be not for me.

'Tis better so perchance (I hate the man
  Who pratingly can maunder ' better so,
If God so wills it :' what God wills, he can
  Have no conception ; of the high, the low
Knows nothing, nor can even comprehend
  What God wills ; if God be, too much for him
To wonder at : he seeks to fix the end
  Of what has no beginning save his whim,
  And drowns himself in quibbles, ere he swim).

Not such my lamentation ; I would give
  All ' betters ' in the future, so that now

The 'good' might be mine own, yea, I could live
  A happy life, with calm contented brow
Far from ambition in a humble home,
  If love dwelt with me, and her gentle hand
Led me from fame, where now my footsteps roam ;
  Ah love were rapture ! Yet I understand
  The greenest swamp may still be treach'rous land :

And tho' its verdure glad me, and I strain
  My clanking fetters to break free and cast
Myself upon its fairness ; and refrain
  Only because stern duty holds me fast
And will not let me go ; yet were it mine
  My raptured eyes would drink its greenery,
Forgetting stars above which faithful shine
  To guide us thro' this fleeting scenery,
  Unto the shores of death's deep mystery.

  [*He rises, goes to the veiled picture and draws away
  the curtain, disclosing* MADAME ROLAND.

My love !  My star !  Set far above my clasp
  In heaven's brightness ! thou canst not descend
To bless my human love, my clinging grasp
  Must close contented on the name of friend ;
A poor name doth it seem when hungry love
  Is longing for love's kiss, and yet most sweet
Of all earth's names, and raisèd far above
  All passion-struggle—ah ! it is not meet
  I should cast down that name which I would greet

My life's best gift !  The name which speaks to me
  Of fairest, brightest hours ; of love and joy

Of perfect peace, unstainèd purity,
  Of happiness without shade of alloy,
Of sympathy in sorrow, of all trust,
  Of myriad gleaming beauties which shall last
Graved on my heart, and when that turns to dust
  A flower-poem shall upspring, and cast
  A crown of memory o'er the time long-past :

Friend ! friend ! my friend ! I'll call thee love no more
  Until time breaks our fetters ; if it be
That merciful unclasping comes before
  I plunge with weary soul in that sad sea
The boundary of our life, then may I rest
  The last brief hours with love ; and I and thou,
Heart clasped to heart, and loving breast to breast,
  May dream of this time gone, and wonder, how
  We lived before, in rapture of the ' now ' !

----

## SCENE II.

*He draws the curtain and again throws himself into
  a chair sunk in thought. Silence for a short
  time, then enter* ROLAND, *who falls exhausted and
  overcome into the nearest seat.*

### ROLAND.

Ah Buzot ! all is lost, all reason gone—
Brute cruelty triumphant ; we may wait
Nor wait long now, our turn will come the next :
The helpless, then their shield—so runs the world—

There lives no gratitude or reverence
In this wild people's heart.   Did we not strive
In the Convention with full heart and voice
To tame this tiger madness ?   Did we not
Urge pardon ?   Mercy ?   And the comment this —
The helpless prisoners surprised and slain,
Nor age, nor sex, nor innocence, none spared.
God ! are these creatures fiends ? They are not men ;
No human blood can circle thro' their veins,
Who calmly gaze on murder, who can drink
The palpitating life of fallen hearts
To pledge their hatred in, and calm decide
In midnight meeting of base treach'rous knaves
The morning massacre.   I have no fear
For us ; they dare not strike, at least not yet,
But madness of the people grows apace :
Louis, his queen and sister, are to fall,
Then comes our turn to feast la guillotine !
This morning he will die ; thou knowest how
We pledged our honour that he should be spared :
We did not speak in riddles, but plain prose,
And yet this victim is torn from our hands,
Our weak faint hands, which have no power to hold—
This our Republic is trailed in the dust,
And all her glorious aims brought down to this
Mere wantonness of murder.—I can hold
(If Louis falls, I wait to hear the news)
My ministry no longer ;—with what pride
I did receive it from the people's hands,
Believing Liberty would blossom fair
Beneath our grand Republic! and yet now
I feel my hands stained with the holding it

F

While such deeds have been done, tho' my firm will
Ever resisted them.

BUZOT.

                    The tune may change
E'en at the last ; the people hardly knows
Its own requirements, and with blinded eyes
Follows dog-like its masters : when they shout
' Down with the traitor !' quick it tears him down,
Most passively brute-like ; but swift is turned
To pity by a word.   Louis must fall,
He sinned too high for pardon ; but his queen,
His sister, must be saved, or—we fall too :
Our Liberty dishonoured, what remains
But gallantly to die on her slain heart !

---

SCENE III.

CAMILLE DESMOULINS *enters and sadly speaks.*

CAMILLE.

He died (poor Louis !) every inch a king,
The majesty of suffering on his brow :
More king-like in his death, than living, he
Constrained the people's tears ; I saw one man
Red-capped, fierce-visaged, crying like a child,
When Louis standing calm, with straight-fixed eyes
And brow serene, unruffled, spread his hands
(Those kingly hands, so weakly thin and white)

Over the surging sea around, and blessed
In clear and silver tones his murderers,
Then bowed before his priest, and laid his head,
As if to slumber, on the guillotine.
Tears fell like rain ; but soon Legendre, Jourdain,
Began the shout, ' Long live our Liberty ! '
' Our brotherhood is safe ! ' (their watchwords still
When brotherhood is dead, and Liberty,
Far worse than death, dishonoured) ; but the cry
Struck on the people's heart.   Each swiftly gazed
To see if traitor tears were still upon
His neighbour's face, and dashed away his own
With louder shouts, and hoarser ' Liberty ! '
They're shrieking for the queen ; we soon shall see
Her woman head struck down ' For Liberty ! '
Elizabeth struck down ' For Liberty ! '
The Gironde guillotined ' For Liberty ! '
I hate the very sound of Liberty !

                [*Exeunt* CAMILLE *and* ROLAND.

---

## SCENE IV.

### BUZOT (*alone*).

#### BUZOT.

If I have e'er had power in my speech—
  If Nature's burning soul dwells in my breast :
If I have strength my flutt'ring tongue to teach
  Impassioned utt'rance for the thoughts exprest—

Let them now serve me, let my words of fire
  Pierce thro' hearts hardened, by the growing might
Of egotism unchecked ; let me aspire
  To hide the sword of death far out of sight,
  And crown once more our Liberty with right !

Oh woman ! I will save thee for the sake
  Of her, a woman fairer than thou art ;
I will before thee stand, and seek to make
  A shield for thee of my own beating heart ;
My voice shall ring distinct thro' trumpet bray
  Straight to the nation's heart, and it shall learn
Again forgotten truths.   I'll make a way
  For mercy in their souls, and they shall turn
And pardon thee with shame and tears that burn !

---

## SCENE V.

*A   Street.   Crowd surrounding tumbril, on which*
MADAME ELIZABETH, *calm and beautiful, is*
*sitting on her way to the guillotine.*

### 1ST CITIZEN.

Louis is dead, the perjured queen is dead,
And thou also wilt be with them, dead too.
How friendly kisses our brave guillotine !
How loving are her lips ! she smiles on all,
The dainty noble, the proud beauty—all
Who seek her she receives, and welcomes them
So warmly they've no taste for other joys.

ELIZABETH (*wearily*).

Friend, I am ready, for no other joys
Can ever glad me more ; my murdered Louis—
My martyr'd sister, smiling, beckon me ;
I hasten to their arms.   Yet—taunt me not,
Me, dying ; think—your own death-hour draws on,
The future hides it yet, and lays bare mine,
And I go forth to greet it with a smile,
Ah, let it be in peace !   I pardon you——
    [*Shouts of women interrupt her*, 'To the guillotine !'

2ND CITIZEN.

'Twere well the drums beat now, and drowned her
        voice,
Lest she, with meek pathetic eyes, corrupt
Our weaker brothers.
    [BUZOT *rushes through the crowd to the side of the*
    *tumbril, springs upon it and speaks passionately,*
    *while it rolls slowly on.*

BUZOT.

Oh citizens ! bid not the drums resound
To drown her voice, which sounding angel clear
In dark days past so often swept all hearts
Into sweet music with its sympathy,
Its pureness of full loving.   Oh ! my friends,
If each of you holds dear one human thing,
As each of you must do, the man lives not
Who brutal, hardened to the whole hard world,
Keeps not still one soft fount of happiness,
One little spot where flower of love up-springs,

Tho' dry and empty of all nourishment
Yet still a blossom, blessing him unknown,
And holding in its beauty germs of good
For the poor heart it dwells in.   By this germ
(The seed of heaven, but needing human rain
Of opportunity to spring to life),
Beseech you friends ! dear friends and countrymen,
My brothers ! hear my voice that pleading deep
For this one life, this helpless woman life,
Still knocks at your heart-portals—let her eyes,
Those meek pathetic wells of beauty, full
Of mercy—pardon, pity, gentleness—
Find echo in your souls—ah friends, dear friends,
Spare her for my sake, brother in the fight
For Liberty, and brotherhood ; dear friends,
For my sake hearken !

### 1ST CITIZEN.

                    Guillotine him too,
He speaks most traitor-like ; he too is one
(Tho' prating glibly of fair Liberty,
Friendship, and brotherhood) of that foul crew
Whose captain, Louis, lately yielded up
Polluted blood . . . tear down the traitor voice !
                    [*Shouts of* ' Down with the traitor !'

### BUZOT.

Nay, hear me brothers ! hear me ! but once more.

### 2ND CITIZEN.

We will not hear thee, tremble for thyself,
Who pities traitors, well may fall with them ;

Beware ! the people watch thee, thou art one
Of that band whose brave words resound alone
With no brave deeds to back them.

LEGENDRE (*hoarsely*).

Drummers, strike up and drown the voice of him
A traitor to the people !
[*Renewed shouting.    Drums strike up, while*
BUZOT *with frantic gestures endeavours to pro-*
*cure a hearing.*

MADAME ELIZABETH.

I know you not, brave Frenchman, who have sought,
With danger to your own, my life to save ;
Poor thanks and prayers are all my fortunes leave
To pay my debt of utter gratitude
To that firm heart and eager stirring voice :
Thanks ! thanks, dear friend ! I little thought to feel
The glow of human greatness sweep my soul
Clear of all petty sorrows at the end,
And clothe me with the joy of sympathy
To meet my God with.   Now farewell, swift go :
I trust a glorious life remains for you
Who bravely have dared death.   [*Holds out her hand.*

BUZOT.
                    I will not go.
Perhaps . . . .

ELIZABETH (*interrupting him*).

Say not 'perhaps ;' 'perhaps' no more
Has any part for me ; if my commands,
Which once were weighty, have not lost all charm

They bore in days gone by, I conjure thee
Swift leave me now ;—I would have no more thought,
Even the purest, of mere earthly things :
I would fix soul and spirit constantly
Upon the heavenly bliss awaiting me.
Suffering is blessèd, easy to forgive
When sin is absent from the suff'ring soul.
My heart holds no place for the personal
Small terror of itself, but brimmeth o'er
With pity for the anguish which o'ertakes
The one who sins, and forces heartlessly
The cup of suff'ring to another's lips.—
Farewell ! go, I command you ; and at once.

BUZOT (*sorrowfully pressing her hand*).

I go then, as you will, reluctantly.
[*Exit* BUZOT. *Procession continues to move on,
and disappears.*

---

## SCENE VI.

ROLAND'S *House. Interior.* MADAME ROLAND. *Enter*
ROLAND, PÉTION, BUZOT, BRISSOT, BARBAROUX,
VERGNIAUD, &c.

ROLAND.

They seek to rob us of our last best gift,
The firmness of our minds, which dare to raise
Still in this madness voices of reproof
Against the murderers of our Liberty :—

They seek to fright us with bare swords and words
Of darkly hinted danger, but in vain ;—
As Romans have we lived, and Romanly,
If need be, we can die.   We have no part
(Since we resigned our Ministry) in death,
Unless it be our own.   Friends counsel flight,
How think you, Pétion ?

---

## SCENE VII.

*LOUVET rushes in pale and terror-stricken.*

### LOUVET.

Fly !   fly !   if you would live, 'tis your one chance.
But now I entered under thick disguise
The Jacobin Club chamber, and I heard
Such hellish words, such most unnat'ral thoughts
Of blood and fire, as made my trembling limbs
Half shudder from their duty ; swift I came
To warn you of your danger : linger not,
Your blood shed by these murderers will be held
A curse to our Republic, and will breed
A race in horror to o'erthrow her state.
Fly ! tarry not, e'en now methinks I hear
The clash of swords, the jangling of fierce oaths,
As those infernals, led by him, the fiend,
(Cursed e'en by nature, mother of us all),
That viper of the gutters, Marat ! he
Who lives that he may slaughter and cut down
All greater and more blessèd than himself

In beauty, intellect, and purity !
Oh tarry not, 'tis madness in such case,
Time long enough to show your bravery
When hope remains to guide you—but fly now !

    [PÉTION *walks coolly to the window and gazes out.*


BARBAROUX.

Fly ? leave our other friends to such a fate ?
Not I, for one ; I'd rather die with them
Than live on, and in after years look back
Upon this night, and think I saved myself
By leaving friends to bear the penalty !
No, never will I fly !   They say each one
Has at some single moment of his life
The power to choose, and on that pivot hangs
His life's renown, or high and holily
To bear himself, or basely ; such he is
For all years after as he makes himself
At that one time-flash : and perchance to us
That moment now has come—to choose, assert
Our dignity in choosing, and make good
Our oft-repeated promises ;—I choose
To stay and die, on-fighting to the last !   [*Sits down.*


    PÉTION (*returning from the window calmly*).

Down pours the rain, 'twill cool our enemies,
And bring their heated brains to calmer thoughts ;
No fear for us to-night ; the patriot herd
Like their warm shelter, and disdain to wet
A sole of patriot foot !   Down pours the rain ;
For this time we may rest, and calm disperse
Unto our sep'rate dwellings ; so, good night.

    [*Exit* PÉTION.

VERGNIAUD (*sadly*).

Our hour is well-nigh come ; I feel the clouds
Of threat'ning fate swift gath'ring, soon they close
And hide blue heaven behind their inky folds ;
Then falls the bolt, and cleaves a fiery way
To waiting hearts, and withers them, and then
Rebounds upon the hurlers, they will fall.
I, close to death, see clearer than before ;
I see the torrent raised, but never stilled,
And bearing with its current friends and foes,
Its leaders and its victims—on—on—on—
Straight with resistless billows, reasonless
And fetterless to death !   The end I see,
The end of all things on the guillotine.—
'Tis the Republic's bitter fate to doom
Her fairest children, her most loving sons,
In blindness unto death :—an ancient saith,
' Whom the eternal gods hate and abhor
They first make mad, and thus self-ruin them
By their own madness : ' thus it is with her,
Our loved Republic ; we have dreamed too much
Perhaps of brotherhood and Liberty,
Forgetting in our studies of old time
The weak inglorious race, who living now,
And aping young-world giants in their acts,
But parody and drag them thro' the mire
Of their base passions, powerless to see
A man must be self-victor, ere he dare
Impose his will on others.
(*After a pause.*)          Farewell friends !
Brissot, Buzot, and Barbaroux, are you
For homeward turning?

ALL THREE.

Yes, we are—good-night.

BUZOT *to* MADAME ROLAND.

Clear hearts can sleep, while traitors watch and fear.

[*Exeunt the four.*

---

SCENE VIII.

ROLAND, MADAME ROLAND.

ROLAND.

I feel a presage of this coming storm ;
A most unusual languor weighs me down,
And nails my spirit to its cross of pain :
No torturing feeling that my own defects
Have drawn this tempest on defenceless heads
Maddens me with regret ; but that calm sigh
The wisest cannot stifle, when on Death
(Death present often in our thoughts and speech,
But realised how seldom !) he must gaze ;
Death, standing resolute, with hand upraised
To strike him down—yet pausing ; 'tis that pause,
And not the stroke, which shakes the firmest heart
As mine is shaken now.

MADAME ROLAND.

Friend, calm thyself ;
'Tis no infirmity, but rather strength,
That thou canst see, and calmly analyse

Thy heart's new weakness ; weakness of the flesh—
Thy never-quailing spirit shines above
This human shudder, proving thee a man,
Tho' noblest, still a man ; not merely hewn
Emotionless and heartless from the stone.
              [*A noise of people outside the door.*

SCENE IX.

*Two* Officers *enter.*

### 1ST OFFICER.

We, under warrant, *(showing a warrant)* hasten to
      arrest
You, Roland, traitor to this land : behold
The pledge of our authority, and yield
Yourself to us, resistance were most vain.
Committee of the Revolution
Have drawn this warrant ; look at it and see
How plainly it commands you, and obey.

ROLAND (*looking at the warrant*).

I yield not to your warrant, and deny
Your vaunted power, and question utterly
Authority you serve ; I will not yield.
Return, and tell those traitors, Roland stands
Firm by the constitution, and dares them
To drag him from its shelter !—I yield not.

### 2ND OFFICER.

We are not messengers 'twixt you and they,
But charged with your arrest.

### MADAME ROLAND.

But are you charged
With violent arrest?   Are your commands
Merely to seize the traitor, or enforce
With sword-point his attendance?   Answer that,
Or your Committee may disown the deed
And leave you with the burden.   How say you?

### 1ST OFFICER.

Our warrant speaks not of resistance here
In plain words certainly ; but still I think
When traitors are at stake, 'tis no light thing
To let them slip for quibble of a word,
An oversight perhaps.

### MADAME ROLAND.

Yet you must take
This oversight upon you, and make good
With your own heads his death, for taken alive
This Roland will not be ; think you then well
If you are warranted to murder him.

### 2ND OFFICER TO 1ST.

'Tis better that we seek a clearer, full,
And more particular authority ;
Thou know'st how ready men are now to leave

The burdens of their deeds on others' backs,
And stand unyoked themselves.

[*Turning to* ROLAND.

We shall return.

[*Exeunt* Officers.

MADAME ROLAND.

Return to find the threatened bird has flown
To safer branches !  Now, my friend, indeed
You must consent to shelter ; I will seek
In the Convention justice ; and will win
Safety for you ere long, but for the time
You must take refuge in some fast retreat
From which if fortune frowns, you swift can wing
Your way from Paris to the Provinces,
And there perhaps (who knows what future holds ?)
Set up our dreamed Republic in the South.
Farewell my husband !  Fare—thee—very well ;
We must part now, I trust to meet again,
But fate lowers darkly.   Let me see thee go,
That I may feel (my mission failing there)
That thou at least art safe.   Oh fare—thee—well !

[*Takes his hand.* ROLAND *draws her towards
him and kisses her.*

ROLAND.

I go.   Farewell, my most dear loving wife,
The truest friend, and sweetest comforter,
A man e'er gloried in !  I'll to our friends
And warn them of this peril ; they *must* fly
If danger darkens. (*Goes out.*)

[MADAME ROLAND, *hastily throwing a shawl over
her shoulders, follows in a few moments.*

## Scene X.

*Street before the* Tuileries, *where the Convention held its sittings, doors closed; crowds of armed men no longer shouting, but sullenly muttering and lounging about; an occasional cry* 'To the Guillotine!' *is heard. Enter* Madame Roland, *her head bare, the shawl flung over her light dress; she hurriedly walks up to the closed doors and tries to enter.*

#### 1ST CITIZEN.

You seek to enter those closed doors in vain ;
The country is in danger, and that cry
Has swelled the tocsin's knell, and locked those doors,
That patriots privately may concert means
To obviate the peril.—Who art thou?
    [Madame Roland *turns from the door and slowly walks away, saying nothing, but gazing sadly at the lowering groups.*

#### 2ND CITIZEN.

She dare not answer ; I suspect that face,
It looks not like our Marat and his friends :
Shall we pursue, and drag her by the hair
Unto the guillotine? What say you, friends?

#### 3RD CITIZEN.

'Twill kiss her soon enough without our hands
To urge the rolling wheel ; her very air
Of gazing straight with deep unflinching eyes
Speaks aristocrat plainly, and will count
Enough for Marat ; we may spare our toil.
    [*Groups pass on sullenly muttering.*

SCENE XI.—ROLAND'S *House.*

MADAME ROLAND (*entering alone*).

It was in vain then that I trusted still
In Liberty's strong shield ; 'tis piercèd thro'
With darts and arrows of men's tyrant wills,
And powerless to guard.—Thank heaven at least
My husband is in safety—he must fly
From this mad Paris hastening to her fall ;
And they, our friends, must fly, our brave young band,
Devoted hearts, and souls, born to aspire
To Liberty star-crowned !  And he my friend,
Whom still with that weak woman-heart of mine
I willingly could cling to ; he must go—
The echo of my soul, my heart expressed
In manhood's type—whose tender voice and thought
I ever felt thrill me with a glow
Of heaven's rapture ; tho' his uttered words
Spoke like mine own of friendship, it was love
Yea, love flame-pinioned, which flashed thro' our speech
The commonest, and lit it with the glow
Our hearts know once, no more ; which darkenèd
We never can relight !  Calm love, indeed,
And high-toned duty may fill up the void
And give us a pure life, contented, brave,
And nobly self-denying ; but the glow
Which shone but once, and sharpened in its light
Our rapture nigh to anguish, lighting up
The highest peaks of life, and making clear
A pathway to the stars, returns no more :
Ah ! happy they who dare enjoy the gleam,

G

And steep their souls in it, and carry it
Undarkened to the end !  Some are so blessed
The mystic glow comes spring-like, whispering
With song of birds, and brooklet's murmuring,
And fills their chainless hearts ; and they enjoy
(Unknowing half their bliss) pure happiness !
But some, and such my fate, are cast upon
A solitary shore, and, down the far
Of heaven's distant blueness, see the glow,
While wide between roll swelling ocean waves
Of duties, fetters—banishing the light,
And leaving dreams alone of what might be !

                  [*She leans back wearily and falls asleep.*

---

## SCENE XII.

*A knock is heard at the door repeated twice or thrice.*

MADAME ROLAND (*starting up half awake*).

What sound was that ?         [*Knocking again heard.*
        Who knocks?  At this hour too—
Enter, whoe'er you be.        [*Two Officers enter.*

1ST OFFICER.

        Where is Roland?
Our duty is now plain, ' Arrest the man,
At sword-point if need be :' behold the words.

MADAME ROLAND.

He is not here ; I know not where he is.

Look at this other warrant, 'tis for you ;
You must prepare, and swiftly, to return
A traitress to the prison ; and your house,
Your goods, and treasures, we sign with the seal
Of the Committee.       [*Begins sealing up desks, etc.*

MADAME ROLAND.

If I deny your warrant, and refuse
To leave my house?

1ST OFFICER.

We straight must drag you thence :
No choice, Madame, better come quietly ;
You can retire, and bid all due farewells ;
We will await you here ; but tarry not,
We've other labours, ere the morning breaks.
      [*Exit* MADAME ROLAND; *the* Officers *continue
      sealing up every thing, even the piano.*

---

SCENE XIII.

*Re-enter* MADAME ROLAND *with little* MARIE *and*
*Nurse carrying a small bundle.*

MADAME ROLAND (*to the* Nurse *aside*).

Leave not my child one instant, until safe
You place her in—her arms ; she will receive
My treasure as a sacred trust, and hold

Her, till I can reclaim.   If nevermore,
Alas !      (*Pressing* MARIE *tenderly to her bosom and
          kissing her.*)
          My darling, may our God send down
A double share of mother-love to her
For my poor orphan ; oh my little one,
The hardest pang is this !   Kiss me, my sweet,
And twine thy little arms round mother's neck—
And so farewell—my child—my own—farewell !
          [*Puts her down gently; the child, frightened at the
          Officers *and her mother's tears, begins to cry.*

MADAME ROLAND (*to* Nurse).

Take her away ; poor little love !   Too young
And tender for such scenes, lull her to sleep,
And tarry not with first blush of the morn
To carry her to (*pauses*) safety.   I will write
A few words of farewell to go with her.
          [*Sits down to the table and writes.*

1ST OFFICER (*aside*).

Treason perhaps, 'neath friendship's frippery.
I must examine.   (*Aloud* to MADAME ROLAND.)   You
          must give the name
Of her, or him, you write to ; in such times,
When treason lurks behind the simplest words,
Suspicion is abroad ; write down the name.

MADAME ROLAND.

I will not.

1ST OFFICER.

          Then my duty plainly is

To tear up that fair letter : will you say
To whom it is addressed ?

MADAME ROLAND.

                 No ; I will tear
It into fragments rather !   (*Tears up the letter.*)
(*To the* Nurse)         Well, you know
All I would say.   Goodbye, my faithful friend !
I leave my heart's best jewel in your care.

   [*Exit* Nurse *weeping and carrying the child;*
     MADAME ROLAND *watches them go, sighs deeply,*
     *then turning to the* Officers.

               I wait your escort.

   [1ST OFFICER *takes her bundle and signs to her to*
     *follow; she does so,* 2ND OFFICER *following*
     *behind.*

## ACT V.

### Scene I.—*The Prison.*

Madame Roland *alone, reading ; she presently lays
down her book and speaks wearily.*

Thro' countless weary days has time rolled on
And stranded me, half hopeless, on the shore
Of gloomy prison life ; my trust, once bright,
Of swift release, and triumph of the right,
And Liberty's return, has worn away
Itself to a mere shadow, and to-day
All hope, all trust, seem but an empty dream.
(*Sighs sadly.*)   I read long since (I hardly know how
        long :
'Tis centuries by heart beats) of my friends
Forced to take refuge in the Provinces,
Or captive in their dwellings, waiting there
The sentence of their virtues, counted crimes
By Liberty's oppressors—oh, I yearn
With longing inexpressible to know
Their fate !—My friends of happy days long past !
My husband has escaped at least arrest,
But homeless wanders, far from wife and child,
And wearily bears ever vain regrets
For Liberty cast down—I cannot bear
                    [*Rises and paces hastily up and down.*

This torture of uncertainty.   How long
Will the dull hours slow drag themselves away
Unto that one I wait for, which shall give
Or death, or li.e, I reck not—so 'tis sure !

---

## SCENE II.

### *Enter* MADAME BONCHAUD.

#### MADAME BONCHAUD.

Friend (I may call you so, for sympathy
Knows no fictitious barriers, and can scale
With grand yet tender wing the dungeon tower,
And dare all peril, or content can bask
With equal joy in safety), I am come
The bearer of good news : 'tis sweet for me
That fortune should make possible to one
Who loves, but never hopes with feeble steps
Of merely loving to attain the height
Unconsciously you bloom on, to give proof
Of boasted friendship with my captive friend
By leading to her presence one of those
Whose glowing souls, strung high for Liberty,
Made rapturous with glory other days.
Buzot, your friend, has prayed me fervently
To overlook all orders, and admit
Him to your prison.

#### MADAME ROLAND.

Humbly do you speak
Of my one solace ; friendship sweeter far

As the poor prison blossom, than as when
It bloomed a rare exotic courting me,
While warm the sun, and calm and blue the sky,
But fading into nothingness when storms
Had swept away my shelter.   Ah ! dear friend,
Your pure unselfishness in serving me
Raises your loving soul above the heights
You place me on ;—as far above my heart
As heaven's arch is over human brows !—
Where is Buzot?   Ah where?   He should be far
Away from here ere now ; I fear for him
So well-known in his greatness.   Bid him come.

------

## SCENE III.

*Exit* MADAME BONCHAUD.   *In a few moments enter*
   BUZOT.   MADAME ROLAND *rises and gives him her
   hand silently, which he as silently holds while they
   gaze sadly at each other, too much affected to speak
   for some moments.*

### MADAME ROLAND.

Buzot, 'tis madness thus to beard grim Death
In his own stronghold ; Paris is no place
For one who loves not slaughter.   Liberty,
Our Liberty, our aim, is now brought down
To a mere formula of 'guillotine.'—
Why hast thou come to me ?   I cannot say
Half that I would, too full and sad my heart ;
Thou knowest my soul's wish, oh tell me swift—

Our friends, my husband—tell me—what their fate?
Those tragic eyes speak death—see, I am calm ;
Life is so short for me, that I can bear
Ages of suffering pressed into a day.
Speak then.

BUZOT (*wildly*).

That I should be the one sought out
By irony of fate to anguish thee !
Oh God, 'tis torture !   Angel ! you are calm—
I see it, as when queen of Girondists
You held your court, and each one of our band
Enshrined you in his heart, religion—
Love, Liberty in one.

MADAME ROLAND.

Speak not of them
In days gone by, but tell me of their fate.

BUZOT.

Then know, the people frantic in its rage,
Lashed into madness by Marat, and he
That Judas of our band, Robespierre,
Surged menace-high thro' Paris and required
Their truest friends should be resigned to them
To wreak their fury on ; and twenty-two
The bravest and most noted were decreed
To stand their trial for treason—some indeed,
With timely warning fluttered from the trap,
Among them Roland, Barbaroux, Louvet,
And Pétion—where they wander I know not,
But our brave South is friendly :—for the rest
They were imprisoned, but their mighty hearts

Gave not one shudder, and the brotherhood
(By Vergniaud their voice) when brought to trial
Spoke with such fiery, burning eloquence
That tears and mercy sprang from stony ground—
The people cried for pity ; and their cause
Was well-nigh won.　Alas! the transient gleam
Of brighter fortune passed, and Vergniaud
Was silenced ; then triumphantly they doomed
The whole band to destruction !—Calm, unmoved
The heroes heard their fate—with one accord
They raised their ringing voices mightily
With ' Long live our Republic !' One alone
As in a swoon down-fell, and voiceless lay ;
It was Valazé, whose fierce love was touched
With martyr longing ; who had joyed to brave
A willing death for Liberty : they found,
When with soft hands and tender they had raised
His fallen body, that brave heart was stilled
For ever ; pierced he lay with dagger yet
Warm with his life-blood, clasped in failing hand,
And martyr rapture of embracèd death
Upon his pallid brow :—the gaze on him
Strung to more vivid tension their tuned souls,
And with triumphant mien and heightened brows
They took their march to death—high rose the song,
The voice of Revolution in its flow
Resistless surging on, the Marseillaise,
Flooded the streets they passed :—as one by one,
The voices failed (the greedy guillotine
Stifling their sweetness into a death-gasp),
Louder and firmer chanted still unmoved
The ever-lessening band ;—Brissot alone

At length stood singing, and with triumph song
He, smiling, met his death.—No more remains
To tell or hear ;—I glory to belong
To such a band ; tho' Girondists no more
May realise their visions, freedom now
Can never die, while tongue lives that can speak
Of such sublimity !—A martyr's blood
Builds ever firmer, with cement of faith
Made manifest in death, its edifice,
And our Republic glorious shall arise
From ashes of her errors, purified,
Made perfect by her woe, and her sons' love.
You can inspire with that flame-wingèd soul
A band more blest, more fortunate than we,
And o'er our martyrs' sacrificial dust
Build Liberty's fair temple, flawless, new,
And wholly indestructible !   For this
I came to-day, to urge your swift escape,
In my name, to our friends ; means I have found
Which shall convey you safely unto them.
Hasten to fly, no time is now to lose.

MADAME ROLAND.

You raise my soul on heroism's wing
Beyond death to eternity; and then
Would drag it down to meanness.   Not in vain
Our friends' sublime example ; I will fall
As firmly as they fell for Liberty.
Seek not to turn my mind; the pyramids
Were easier hewed down than I escape,
Escape, and leave my loving tender friend,
The only solace of my dungeon life,

And thee, the brightener of my happy hours,
The strengthener of my soul, my spirit's star,
To suffer in my stead ?   Listen, Buzot ;
You cannot think me poor enough for this !
You shall not hold me low enough for this !


BUZOT.

Low ? poor ?   My nature's queen, I hold you poor ?
You cannot see my heart, how fervently ·
I cherish you, the angel of my soul,
My life's good genius !   I can ne'er forget
The weakness once you pardoned, and made me
Look thro' the mist of passion, and see clear
Behind the moment's longing, noble thoughts,
And higher aims for seeking ;—if indeed
I have done aught worth mem'ry, 'tis to you,
To you alone, I owe it ; I am blessed
In that my fate denying me all else
Has given me the precious privilege
Of dying at your side.   You will not fly ?
I also will remain—'tis better so—
I am content—nay, chide not—I am firm
Unmoved as your own soul.


MADAME ROLAND (*firmly*).

                              'Tis frenzy, thus
To jest at human barriers ; while they stand
We may o'erlook, but never can ignore :
Their shadow darkens every path in life,
While with their fetters cobweb fine and soft
They hold society in union, tho'
They cripple some, yet to the general flock

They prove most strong protection, and hold back
The spoiler from his prey with iron bands
Of what will the world think? or say? or do?
Were you my brother, ah, how willingly
I could cling to your side ; or were that name
Of closer union yours—but as it is,
Tho' my heart feels the sweetness and leaps up
In eagerness to drink at friendship's spring ;
Yet my firm soul denies it, and casts down
The sparkling draught, sweet, yes, but poison-
   charged !—
No, Buzot, you must fly ; in other lands
Pursue the aims you strove for in your own,
And find in other eyes the gift you seek
But vainly here in mine.   Death is too near
For any self-deception.   I may say
Without a blush, had life been different
I could have loved you, and for love resigned
All other thought, or hope, or aim, but you—
If this be any comfort, take it now.
We never meet again ; farewell, Buzot!
                    [*He makes gestures of dissent.*
Nay, strive not, you must leave me ;  I have need
To send some papers of great moment, swift
Unto my husband ; you must fly, and bear
Them safely to his hands.   Farewell, Buzot !
                    [*Gives him a packet.*
Remember all our aims, and strive for truth,
For Liberty and freedom, to the end.
Farewell again.   Farewell ! farewell !   I pray
For my own sake, oh leave me ! leave me now.
      [*Falls exhausted into a chair and covers her eyes*

*with her hand.* BUZOT *kneels down at her side
and kisses the other hand.*

#### BUZOT.

Farewell my star !   I go to do thy will,
But I return, to rescue thee or die !     [*Exit* BUZOT.

---

### SCENE IV.

MADAME ROLAND *remains motionless for a short time,
then raises herself and speaks, brokenly at first, but
waxing clear and strong as her thoughts change.*

#### MADAME ROLAND.

So the last pang is over, and now I
Must fortify myself to stand before
The murderers of my friends and Liberty
With unmoved presence, dauntless in their sight,
And hear unflinching basest calumnies
Hurled on my name.   Yet I am strong to bear,
And I will show a woman can be brave,
Tho' standing shelterless in the fierce heat
Of tyrants' passions ; let them do their worst !
I can but die ; they rob me of my life,
But that eternal thirst for Liberty,
That high endeavour for humanity,
That striving to make clear to human hearts
The lowness of their aims, and in the strife
To lighten them enlightening my own
With flash of inspiration which all work—

The humblest, and the lowest as men hold
With arbitrary will that sets a bound
To work a gentleman may venture on,
And yet not soil his hands, while baser clay
Must toil in lower fields ; all work I say,
If truly laboured at with heart and soul,
Not merely superficial dallying,
Brings inspiration to the labourer
And blesses him with sense of comforting,
And crown of satisfaction ; so he sees
The eternal gods in common daily things,
And clearly reads in wayside flower and leaf
A higher truth, a sweeter sense of right,
Of all due balancing of properties,
And true proportion which is beauty's law—
Than any gentleman who lounges on
Thro' life ; too grand he thinks (poor brainless fool)
To mar those fair white hands with labouring,
Or tan the pale skin on his snowy brow
By sweat of work and sunlight's wandering.—
I feel that I have toiled, and now the time
Has almost come when I can toil no more,
But this sweet sense of full accomplishment
They cannot take away ; they can but doom
Me to a swifter glory.—I am strong,
Yea eager, for the combat.—I will plead
With all my strength, and Liberty shall light
Me now, as ever, to the goal of life.

## SCENE V.

JAILOR *enters.*

##### JAILOR.

They call for you, and wait below to lead
You to the Tribunal.   Will you descend?

##### MADAME ROLAND.

Yes, gladly ; yield me but a moment's grace ;
I'm still enough the woman to take count
Of ruffled hair, and carelessness of dress,
Or misplaced ribbon 'mid life's tragedy.
Bid them wait for me but a little time,
I will attend them willingly.

##### JAILOR.

I will.                      [*Exit.*

---

## SCENE VI.

MADAME ROLAND *retires to an inner room and quickly
returns dressed in white, her long dark hair floating
in curls over her shoulders.*

##### MADAME ROLAND.

Now I am ready.   'Tis a foolish thought,
A vestige of life's childhood, to connect
The white robe with a sense of innocence;
And so the prejudice, or vanity,

I know not which, has led me in this hour,
This supreme hour of fate, to don the garb
Which speaks of childhood and of purity.

JAILOR (*re-entering.*)

I grieve to hasten you.   Will you descend?
The officers refuse to tarry more.

MADAME ROLAND.

I will.   Tho' death awaits me, yet I go
With no weak trembling ; no fear of my fate,
But glory far beyond it guides me now.
        [*Exeunt* MADAME ROLAND *and* Jailor.

---

SCENE VII.

*The Tribunal.*   President, *seated ; various Members of
    Revolutionary Committee ;* Public Accuser.   *Enter*
    MADAME ROLAND *behind the bar of the accused.*

PUBLIC ACCUSER.

This woman, Marie Roland, is accused
Of plotting treason with the Girondists
Against our liberties ; to seize the power,
And guide the reeling vessel of the State
Into the quicksands of their party ends.
She holds communion with those traitors, and
Is cognisant of where the rebels lurk.—
I therefore on these pleas do summon her
To this Tribunal to show cause and proof
Why death be not awarded to her crimes.

H

PRESIDENT.

Speak, Marie Roland, answer if you can.

MADAME ROLAND, *in a firm and clear voice, with dignified yet enthusiastic gestures, speaks.*

I count these accusations, and these crimes
With which you charge me, glory ; and declare
I have no feeling I should blush to own
With all the world for witness.—Well I know
You count my union with the Girondists
The blackest of my deeds ; 'tis that alone
Of which I am accused ; I joy to hear
Such honour from your lips, and openly
Confess the proudest of my life's fair gifts
Was friendship of this Gironde, whose high aims
And noble struggles for true Liberty,
And our Republic's welfare, such as ye,
Who strive alone for empire and not right,
Cannot appreciate, or comprehend.
Think not, I, helpless, here by force was drawn.
No : friends were true, and would have made for me
A passage of escape, but that I scorned
To take advantage of their friendliness
And lure them into danger; I saw well
The path of duty, honour, led me here ;
Duty, in that I would not injure those
In whose care I was placed, who changed for me
A prison to a home, and solaced me
For loss of freedom, by the countless small
But sweet'ning daily actions which make life

A blessing or a curse : honour—in that
If I had fled, the low malicious tongues
Of stinging insects, waiting warily
To note each flaw, each weakness, would have seized
The moment, too propitious to be lost,
To sting away my fair fame, and make black,
With double meanings and contemptuous ' ifs,'
My innocence and truth.—I stand alone
And helpless in your hands, yet tremble not,
Nor shrink before my doom. My country needs
One more example, and I offer it
Myself, with willing heart, and leave to you
Completion of a sacrifice, for which
The victim was self-offer'd :—afterwards,
When calmer days have cooled the people's blood,
They may turn, and reproach you with my death ;
A woman's death, whose only crimes were these :
That having friends whose faithfulness she knew,
She scorned betrayal ;—and to mighty truth
Her homage rendered, tho' death was the price !—
But souls like mine, who commune with the great
Of other ages, see beyond their own ;
And heed not in the bright'ning future's light
The darkness of the present ;—noble hearts
Forget themselves, and in the growing might
Their sacrificial blood gives to the race
They die for, find their best reward,—and I
Am ready thus to fall ! Oh may I be
The last of those who conquer human love,
And frailty, by the strength of intellect,
And mount unmoved the scaffold guilt and fear
Have doomed them to !

### PRESIDENT.

We still may pardon you,
If you declare with accurate and true
Description Roland's hiding-place.   You know
(How should you not?) his refuge ; answer then.

### MADAME ROLAND.

There is no law which forces human hearts
To sacrifice the nature in their depths,
And tear out all the clinging loveliness
Of earth's affections ;—if I know, or not,
My husband's refuge, that you well may judge,
But never from my lips shall sound proceed
Which brings him into danger.—I can die,
Despising, scorning death ! yea, limb from limb
Can be torn at your pleasure ; but in vain
You strive to wring from my resolvèd mind
The utterance of weakness.   You but know
The anguish of the body, nor can dream
What noble souls feel well, that fleshly pain
The most intense and vivid you can give,
Yea, pressed down till the poor humanity
Sinks quailing into nothingness,—is naught
Compared with that dread torture of the mind
Which feels that it has sinned, and cast away
Its heritage for safety.

### PRESIDENT.

Then, since you,
With obdurate proud will, disdain to yield
Your country service, by revealing here

The lurking-place of traitors, we must doom
You to submit to chastisement of crimes ;
E'en death, for treason against Liberty.
You, Marie Roland, we condemn to die !

### MADAME ROLAND.

You crown me with your doom !   I joy to hold
The hand of fellowship in death with those
(The noble hearts, the most undaunted souls)
You counted worthy death ; and I shall strive
To die like them, unmoved and willingly.—
We prove our right to liberty, who dare
Courageously meet death.          [*Curtain falls.*

---

## SCENE VIII.

*The Prison.*   MADAME ROLAND *alone, calm and
resolved.   Her voice changes as the changing thoughts
sweep across her mind.*

### MADAME ROLAND.

To-morrow then I die ; yet I feel calm,
As if the weary days were dragging on
Still to an unknown bourne ; as if my mind
Saw stretching far in fading distant blue
Long years of living, and not one short night.
E'en yet I cannot realise how near
The great awak'ning is ; and dimly feel
A shadow fading into brightening
Of soul and mind, half fetterless from flesh ;

And know, yet cannot grasp, a mighty truth
The veil of life (transparent at the end)
Still keeps behind its folds, yet half reveals.
    Farewell sweet life, farewell !
          However good and fair
          Thou now dost seem to me,
          Yet I must from thee tear
          Myself, not willingly,
            But of compulsion ;
          And yet I weep not now
          As those who fear to die,
          Ah no ; the fear of death
          Has long ago gone by,
          And I can yield my breath
            With no impulsion
          To 'scape from these bare walls.—
          The grief that o'er me falls
          Is personal no more,
          But fully abstract now,
          For I have reached the door
          Which opens to death's hand,
          And with no sinking brow
          Can wholly understand
          What I before but dreamed,
          Tho' my dim visions seemed
          An echo from that shore
          I tread now evermore.
Thoughts flood my soul, beyond control
  Of language, spring they winged to speech ;
Oh give me time, in measured rhyme
  That I may leave them, I beseech !

Ah ! I have fought with word and thought
  For glorious, sacred Liberty ;
And from my youth have sought out truth
  And grasped the noble and the free.
My life is sweet ; and tiny feet
  Make music in its quiet halls.
My husband's voice bids me rejoice,
  And softer on my spirit falls
Than angel's tone ; but now alone
  They lead me forth to die with morn,
And he is far who was my star
  And soon will tread this earth forlorn.
We had a dream, and like a stream
  Of glory from the sky it fell,
To give this earth a second birth,
  And lo ! it proves a funeral knell.
And yet I know, tho' now I go
  A martyr for that dream's decline,
There shines a morn (yet to be born)
  When my vain dream a truth will shine !
We are not merely shadows in the motion
  Of star that links to star,
Incapable of personal emotion—
  Just tossed down from afar ;
No ; in each one there lives a will sufficing
  To guide him to his goal,
If he but scorn the world's vain voice enticing
  Him to deny his soul.
Each in himself contains his own fruition,
  Each to perfection tends,
If he but follow Nature's pure tuition,
  Which inspiration lends

To each true heart who follows her kind leading ;
  She never can betray,
But ever higher mind and spirit feeding
  With thoughts of perfect day,
Of perfect knowledge, perfect peace abiding—
  Life's mysteries no more
In souls prophetic, agonies providing
  While groping at the door ;
The door which death alone can fully open,
  Tho' sometimes from afar
A radiance gleameth, very faint and broken
  As from a distant star :
It shineth now on me ; and yet one thought
Will dim its brightness.    Ah ! my fair young child,
How will the harsh world treat thee when I'm gone?
Will it press down a crown of thorns on thee
To crush out thy brow's brightness?   Will it curse
The Roman spirit in thy brave young heart
(Thy Roman father's gift), and make thee drink
The vinegar and gall prepared for those
Who dare unveil its falsehoods ?—who can say ?—
Perchance thy path may be 'mid the deep grass
Of life's low pasture lands, o'ershaded e'er
By stately trees ; not envying their state,
But joying in their shadow ; while the flowers
Which gem thy life are simple, yet so sweet
They drown all thought of wider, higher blooms :
The daisy's golden eye is thy life's star,
And homely murmur of the breeze-blown blades
Lulls thee to slumber, while unheard above
Rolls on the stately music of the spheres,
Unknown to thee, and therefore undesired.—

I cannot wholly wish that thine should be
A lot like this, and yet—'tis happiest,
As common minds count bliss.   The poet soul
Alone can soar, and fully knowing still
The beauty of the low, and all the bliss
Found in the shadow, yet dares seek the high,
All careless of the glare which burns his soul
Into a keener glory by its pain ;
And gives him for the earthly laurel wreath
A crown of suffering :—while life's homely joys,
The pleasure of the green grass, zephyr-stirred—
The violet's meek perfume—tender sounds
Of streamlet rippling, and the low of kine—
And thousand twinkling joys of wayside life,
Are his to feel, to glad in, and to sing—
But never to enjoy ; his poet heart
Sees but the poetry, and never tastes
(It cannot, 'tis impossible) the prose :
Thank heaven it is impossible !   A soul
Tuned to the stars could never make its home
Where clasping bind-weed hides the heaven's blue,
And rises just so high as loving hearts
Support it, but again falls to the earth,
And twines itself content round stone, or twig,
Or common wreck of life ;—wilt thou be thus,
My daughter?   Oh my darling, may thy path,
Howe'er it be, ne'er leave bright truth's highway !
And may'st thou, like thy mother, gladly fall
For Liberty and right !   May thoughts of death
Be powerless to turn thy heart away
From following, honour-led, thy father's aim !
Oh God, send down all blessings on my child,

My own, own child, my darling ! and make her
Worthy her name, her country, and her God !—
I leave her in Thy hands ; my faith is sure,
Tho' sav'ring not of dogmas harshly held
By canting priest and persecuting Church ;
No ! the eternal spirit, fetterless,
And boundless in its flight as the wide arch
Of unimaginable space above,
Bearing sun, moon, and stars within our ken
As but an atom in its boundlessness,
Can never be chained down to one alone
Of countless lights in this dark world of ours !
The Church's kindly beams are shed around,
And in their little circle make a glow
To warm tired hearts by, who with youthful haste
Have torn themselves in struggles with mankind,
Or bruised their wings with combats in the dark
Of yet unfledgèd spirits—childish souls
Have need of childish nourishment ;—I say
This not with scorn, or with the pride of one
Who thinks herself above such comforting,
But as a truth—slow-dawning—still a truth :—
For those without the circle of the Church,
Souls star-aspiring, needing earthly props
No more to reach the heavens, her little light
Seems glimmering but to make more visible
The darkness of her path :—for those, I hold,
Who bear within their spirits evidence
Of their high destiny, nor need a man
Far lesser than themselves (in that his mind
Feeds on the leavings of past greater souls
Who long ago saw truth, and left a sign

Of what she said to them ; but not to bind
The coming hearts, but merely indicate,
The mind must from itself evolve its gods
Or follow blindly false ones !) to make clear
God's will to them (a lesser god than they);
For these to bow their shoulders to the yoke
Were merely mockery, and I held it so ;
And struggled free from Church, and creed, and priest,
But not from God ; no !  My immortal soul
Knew that its inspiration dwelt not here ;
And looking round on nature, saw with eyes
Clear opened to behold, each plant, and bird,
Or humble creeping life, slow-working still
On to a definite end with no false aim,
But merest germ of longing in a shoot
To twine round something, teaching it to turn
In subtle revolution, seeking rest,
Until it finds completion, when again
Its journey is repeated, on, on, on,
The ceaseless striving of humanity
In lower type clear-speaking—so my mind
Raised step by step, and strengthening as it grew
Towards the stars, by study of the earth,
Felt that its yearnings must like nature's throbs
Speak possibilities of inner life
Out-blossoming some time ; and cast about
In twining convolutions (like the shoot)
To find support for climbing ; and drew forth
From treasure store of boundless intellect,
An image (faint and dim, but growing still
More bright and clear, for gazing of clear eyes)
Of that eternal, reigning loveliness ;

Truth manifest—yea, God !—such is my faith ;
And having this sublime belief, shall I
Tremble to die ? a moment's agony,
Too great a price to pay for endless bliss ?
No ; I feel raised above all human pain,
My spirit e'en now soars, and with foretaste
Of dreams' fulfilment, scoffs at earthly bands.
Would that the hour were come ! I could die now
With rapture !   May my soul resigned and calm
Thus bear herself to-morrow !   I will rest
This weary body, lest its humanness
Drag down my spirit at the final hour.
Sleep, sweet and gentle, under thy kind wing
I shelter me ; be merciful, and swift
Waft all my waiting into strengthening.

> [*Speaks towards the end slowly and drowsily, then
> gradually falls back asleep.*

---

## SCENE IX.

*Street with guillotine erected.   On one side gigantic
statue of Liberty.   Executioner ; scattered groups of
people with sullen brows occasionally muttering dis-
contentedly.   Tumbril appears in sight, with
MADAME ROLAND and an Old Man.   MADAME
ROLAND in white as at the Tribunal ; Old Man
stretching out his hands to the people.*

### OLD MAN.

Oh brothers, save me !   I am old, and weak,
I cannot injure you, oh let me live !

I dare not die, I fear—I cannot die !
Oh brothers, be but merciful this once,
And spare my old defenceless, harmless life !

### 1ST CITIZEN.

Some sport is here—a man afraid to die ;
The first one of the batch !   Let's follow him.

### 2ND CITIZEN *to* Old Man.

A life like yours (so very near its close)
Would never pay for saving ; but at least
We will see last of you.  [*To* 3RD CITIZEN] Keep close,
    keep close.

### 3RD CITIZEN.

How the crowd presses ! 'tis the woman there
Who draws all eyes upon her.

### MADAME ROLAND (*to* Old Man).

            Friend, why fear
To close your span of life ? one moment more
Or less of living cannot conquer death ;
In Nature's course you must have perished soon ;
Calm yourself then ; 'tis but an instant's pain,
With everlasting rest beyond the stroke.
I too shall die—my doom is first to fall.
Look on me, do I tremble? be a man !
You must have looked on death with unmoved eye
In battle-fields ere now.

### OLD MAN.

            Aye, that I have !
But this slow-growing horror strikes me down,

I cannot conquer it.—You die the first,
And will not see the anguish of my fall ;
But I shall feel the quivering of your heart
As the knife falls, and doubly suffer death,
In witnessing, ere I can suffer it !

MADAME ROLAND.

You fear to see my spirit quail at last,
And nature shrink at the dread agony ?
Ah friend, my strength is greater ; I can bear
To see you fall, nor sigh—and then calm mount
The scaffold and firm die :—your turn shall be
The first then.   Courage ! die for Liberty
Without a groan ; 'tis but a moment's pang.
     [Old Man *falls back with a sob of relief. Tum-*
       *bril stops at the foot of the guillotine.* Executioner
       *advances to* MADAME ROLAND.

EXECUTIONER.

Being a woman, 'tis your privilege
To suffer death the first.

MADAME ROLAND.

                But I would choose
To waive that privilege, and render up
My turn to this poor man : let him die first.

EXECUTIONER.

I cannot change my orders for a whim.

MADAME ROLAND.

But can you have the heart to take from me

My woman's right of choosing? 'tis the last
Of my free actions, do not then deny
Me the poor granting of a woman's wish.
Lead this man tenderly ; so old and weak
With fighting battles for his murderers ;
And hasten to abridge the agony
Weak souls feel in suspense.

> [*Executioner half unwillingly turns to* Old Man
> *and takes hold of his arm* ; Old Man *does not
> move.*

EXECUTIONER.

                Come, waken now ;
You soon will sleep enough.
(*Shakes him roughly.*)       Why ! what is this?
He's dead already ; I may spare my toil.
(*Drops his arm,* Old Man *falls motionless to the ground.
To* MADAME ROLAND.) You have your privilege
against your will.

MADAME ROLAND.

Poor human creature ! he has gone to rest ;
The fear of death has stifled in his heart
All power of life. (*To* Executioner.) I thank you
for the grace
You rendered me, tho' vain.

> [*She mounts the scaffold with a firm undaunted step,
> and turning towards the statue of Liberty,
> gravely bows.*

MADAME ROLAND (*to statue*).

Farewell my goddess ! I shall greet this morn
True Liberty unveiled :—her image here,

Standing with calm unruffled brow to see
The death of all who loved her, is a type
Of earthly Liberty, set up to cloke
The basest crimes with plausibility !
Yet, Liberty, thou blessest with thy look
Of high resolve, and dauntless suffering,
My dying hour ; I have lived as thy child,
And die now as thy martyr !   Farewell life !

> [*Curtain falls as she stands with clasped hands,
> and eyes upraised to the statue.*

# POEMS

THE moonlight lay calm on the folded mountains,
    And touched their whiteness with silver shine ;
The breezes swept o'er the echoing fountains ;
    Earth's whispered beauty looked half divine :

And the star-god, gazing while onward singing
    His chariot rolled thro' the ether's blue,
Felt a dream-like yearning to hear the ringing
    Of earth-bells lost from that distant view.

He knew but the moonlight rapture of beauty,
    Nor dreamed of the darkness ere the morn ;
For right is desire, and pleasure is duty,
    In that fair world to which he was born :

So leaving the glory, and music blisses
    He ever tasted, so never knew,
He slid down the rapturous clinging kisses
    Of breezes moon-driven the blueness thro'.

A shadow of sorrow, a dim regretting
    (As moment's darkness on moon's fair light)
Fell over his spirit, as onward setting
    His will in his wings, he took his flight.

I 2

He passed thro' the dreamy stillness, swift-weaving
  Such visions of earth-love rapture clear
As only are known in the world he was leaving,
  And cannot even be dreamed of here.

He floated away, while his star grew dimmer,
  And sighed its chorus with waning voice,
As the spheres rolled on, and its weeping glimmer,
  Was lost, since its god had made his choice ;

And chosen the sad-browed earth for his dwelling,
  Forsaking his glory, love, and star ;
The white clouds marvelled, and wept in the telling,
  With rain down-falling on us afar.

But the star-god recked not the tender weeping
  Of clouds, his friends in the days gone by ;
Still onward he slid thro' the moonlight, keeping
  His watch on the earth, forgetting the sky.

At last on the mountain's fair silver foldings,
  That mystic fretwork of light and shade,
He thought he could trace clear his dim beholdings ;
  And passion of fragrant wings delayed.

But as his chilled feet the sharp coldness tasted
  (Earth's coldness piercing through heaven's dreams)
Of the snow peaks for whose sake he had hasted
  From star-world rapture, and angel beams,

A doubt struck his soul with prophetic warning,
  That earth might be fair, yet hard and cold ;

For moonlight was fading, and cloudy dawning
   Half froze the fragrance of star-wings' fold.

'Oh hills, whose wild beauty, my spirit's longings
   For something beyond its tasted bliss,
Answered with dreamy yet far wafting songings
   Which spoke to me clear with breeze's kiss ;

'Did my soul receive your dim message wrongly?
   Speak to me now, I have come to you ;
For my heart is sad, and my pinions strongly
   Flutter to soar the moonlight thro'.'

The star-god listened for answer, deep-pleading
   With glorious sadness of his eyes,
While the silver faded ; and sun rose, leading
   Morn to her place 'mid the darkling skies.

Then the mountains quivered, and half-revealing
   Beneath the realist sun their brows,
With no moonlight glory of poet healing
   To hide the bareness which night allows :

Said sadly : 'Oh star-god, no word or whisper
   Came from us floating to you afar ;
It might be the streamlet, the valley's lisper,
   Whose voice reached thro' space, your distant star :

'Seek not in silence of mountains, upraising
   Their heads to listen against the sky,
But in prattling plains for ever praising
   Their greenness and beauty, with no sigh

' For the heights they reach not, nor in their vision
　　Dream of reaching; too lowly their soul;
It is but a high mind whose prevision
　　Can seek the high in its wished-for goal !

' Too great our wild longing, and patient yearning
　　For something we know not, yet can feel
Is waiting in space for our future learning,
　　But which must be known ere it can heal:

' Too mighty our patience for word of wailing,
　　Rapture of beauty, or song of love ;
Calm, unmoved and sublime, with never-failing
　　Expectant peaks we gaze on above.

' Seek in the valley the streamlet's low tinkle,
　　Murmuring " follow me " to its shore ;
Or seek the wide ocean whose brow no wrinkle
　　Bears on its fairness for evermore.'

The star-god listened, and calm at the ending
　　With wondering brow he gazed below
To the plain, and with footsteps slow descending
　　And longings cast upward did he go.

Green lay the valley, with bright sunlight waking
　　Over each dew-laden leaf and bloom;
While the birds rejoicing greeted morn breaking,
　　Which spake to them but of conquered gloom ;

And the star-god knew that their voices gladdened
　　A scene of beauty, and hoped again,

With a soul rebounding from words that saddened
To find his dream of the mountains vain :

And he sang with the magic rhythm of glory
The stars repeat to each passing cloud :
' Ah little birds, tell me the joyous story
I heard in my distant world, and loud

Echoing thro' all the brightness and wonder
Of boundless space did its notes resound,
Till I left my star for the song-world under
And on snow mountain my footsteps found ;

' But the hills denied what my fervent dreaming
Had crownèd them with, and bade me seek
In the valley's streamlet my vision's gleaming,
And not on the silent mountain peak :

' Tell me, oh gay birds ! your sweet meaning clearly :
What is the rapture you lured me to ?
Come to me closely, and whisper me nearly
The secret which drew me down to you.'

But the birds still singing, light answered, straying
The while thro' the green leaves fresh with dew ;
' Oh star-god, we know not your cause for praying,
We never whispered or sang to you :

' We twitter with rapture, and sing souls afire
At glory of blossom, fruit, and leaf—
We some of us into the blueness aspire,
And some of us weary earth with grief;

' But no voice of ours 'mid the stars on-singing,
    Could ever be heard thro' distant space :
Seek farther, oh star-god ! the music ringing
    In thy dreams of earth has here no place.'

' Oh greenness of valleys, flower-besprinkled !
    Tell me, oh tell me, was yours the tone
Which rang thro' the stillness, and silver tinkled
    'Mid rapture-music to me alone ? '

Smiling, the sweetness of blossoms repeated,
    ' Star-god, seek farther, no tone of mine
Could draw thee away from thy glory, heated
    By dreams of beauty and love divine.'—

Then with sorrowful steps, the star-god pondered,
    ' Where shall I find my dream's clear voice ? '
Till he came to a stream, which rippling wandered
    And chanted away, ' Rejoice, rejoice ! '

' At last then 'tis found,' said the star-god singing ;
    ' Oh brooklet, whisper me, why rejoice ?
For your joyous song thro' the ether ringing
    Drowned to my ears every other voice ;

' And lured me away to the mystic glowing
    Of beauty I felt behind that tone ;
I have sought but vainly for further knowing,
    But now I hear it is yours alone ;

' Tell me the meaning, for I am so weary
    Of asking vainly all this while ;

And my soul finds darkness of earth more dreary
    For memory of a past star-smile.'

Then the brooklet murmured, ' You question vainly ;
    The meaning I know not nor can tell
Of my happy song, it speaks to me plainly
    Of rain-drops which in the night down-fell ;

' When the pattering blessings dropping sweetly,
    Have given my happy heart a voice,
I sing and flow on to the ocean fleetly
    With joyous refrain, " rejoice ! rejoice ! "

'Come, follow me, follow me, till my flowing
    Is lost in the whelming ocean tide ;
For the ever-restless may all unknowing
    Have lured thee to her echoing side."

So the star-god followed the brooklet's leading
    Till its voice was drowned in mighty roar
Of the surge resistless, as shoreward speeding
    It leapt to his feet ; and then once more

With his voice sad ringing he questioned, craving ;
    ' Oh mighty ocean ! was yours the song
Which rang thro' the moonlight and white clouds, waving
    Me from my star-world to earth along ? '

' Seek farther yet, for thy dream's solution,
    No voice of mine spoke of rapture clear ;
I know not that song, and stern resolution
    Is all my mission to teach or hear.—

' When ships down-sinking, and prayers and groaning
   Ring o'er my waves 'mid the tempest's glare,
Dost dream I think aught of thy brightness roaming
   In blueness and glory thro' the air?

' No ;—yet in the silence of moon down-shining,
   When my restless ocean-heart is still,
A dawning idea which is half divining—
   A shadow of stars—my waters fill ;

' And I murmur, flowing with tender sweetness,
   " Oh shadows, whose light my spirit knows,
Will time ever come when with full completeness
   The sea will rest from its wrecks and woes?"

' But the stars and the moonlight leave me ever
   Without a word, when the morning beams,
And a song of rapture has blossomed never
   From my soul whose torment endless seems.

' Seek in the ancient mysterious hushing
   Of forests primeval, wise, and old,
The clear voice of rapture and glory rushing
   Till space was flooded, and thy star told.'

Then the star-god turned from ocean denying
   The voice whose whisper had drawn him down,
Till he missed heaven's music for earth's sighing
   And won but regret for his lost crown ;

And came to the many-voiced, waving wonder
   Of greenness twinèd in weaving fold,

And parted the gleaming branches asunder
  Whose beauty his soul joyed to behold ;

And he gazed entrancèd, and half forgetting
  The prayer his voice so often told,
While the murmur swept o'er his rapt soul, setting
  Each separate thought in frame of gold ;

For the yellow sunlight crept thro' the tracing
  Of convolute branch's bloomy spray,
Whose scarlet blossoms flame-tipped, up-facing
  The god with their glory, bade him stay.

' Forest mysterious, whispering treasure
  Of wisdom my spirit craves to know ;
Beseech you, reveal me the secret measure
  Your swinging rhythm wafts to and fro :

' I have sought (but vainly) on crowned snow mountain
  That voice and beauty which filled my dream;
Have sought them in valley, and ocean's fountain—
  In glad bird-songs and murmuring stream :

' But alas for my seeking ! it hath met ever
  Denial swift given in refrain ;
Tell me, oh forest ! will questioning never
  Give me fruition, or dream, again ? '

Then the mystic forest, so gray and hoary,
  Whose wondrous voices are only known
To the poet who weaves them in his story
  And makes their longings and love his own ;

Answered the star-god with green light thro' shining
　　Emerald-glory 'tween bough and grass,
Slow-weaving the song of the leaves entwining
　　In verses where sunlight and shadow pass :

' Star-god, we cannot reveal to your pleading
　　Wisdom and beauty you yearn to grasp ;
For the voice you heard, and the dreams down-leading,
　　Are not for a mortal hand to clasp ;

' But we are so old that the fading glory
　　Of earth's rare beauty and fervent love
Seems but a repeating of one sad story
　　Now shrieked below, now murmured above :

' We see the myriad life 'neath our branches
　　Bud and blossom, or fruit, and then die,
Just as fate threatens it, or fortune chances,
　　Or storm or sunlight reigns in the sky ;

' And we know the striving and helpless longing
　　Of lives with nerve-tension strung so fine
That it quivers beneath mere human songing,
　　And dreams that earth-beauty is divine !

' Star-god, no voice merely *objective* singing
　　Could e'er have drawn thee from bliss afar
'Twas *subjective* poet-heart in thee ringing,
　　Inspired by the beauty of thy star :

' Never on earth will the realisation
　　Of thy fair vision and hope be found,

For thou must on-struggle without cessation
 Thro' thy sharp longings, the earth-life round :

' 'Twas the light of thy poet soul uplifting
 Its own rare beauty, and shedding far
Its glory across the blueness, and gifting
 Earth with a sweetness beyond thy star.

' Oh poet ! sing on when the darkness closes,
 And moon arises with mystic light ;
Sing sadly beneath thy crowning earth-roses
 For blisses dreamed of, but lost from sight :

' Sing on, oh star-god ! with yearning and wonder
 Of glory and rapture in the blue,
When the stars sweep on, and are cast asunder
 But swift to return their mazes thro' :

' Sing all the passionate throbbing of sorrow
 An earth-life, born to the stars must feel ;
But sing, ah ! sing on of that dawning morrow
 Which bears in its bosom strength to heal.

' Enter the hard world, oh star-god and poet !
 As it is now, not as in thy dream ;
Too soon thou wilt learn to dread it, and know it,
 Careless of beauty, or love, or beam—

' Ever seeking its weeds of selfish pleasures,
 Passing all flowers of noble deeds ;
Counting its mean worthless baubles its treasures,
 And recking not of its high souls' needs :

' Crushing the genius with iron fetters
    Of custom—mode—and striving to burn
Into his bright soul with blood-red, harsh letters,
    " No place in our world for souls who yearn

' " For aught beyond our most usual living :
    No ; raise us corn for our bread alone,
And prate not of rapture which comes in giving,
    Let each one firm grasp, and keep his own."

' Enter this hard world, oh star-poet ! fated
    To suffer its torments, and make clear
To weaker souls in its meshes belated,
    That glory exists beyond the " here " :

' Enter, and struggle for earth-food to nourish
    Star nature touched with the earthly need ;
Strive where man's industry most high doth flourish,
    But struggle also his soul to lead

' Up wonder to fragrant rapture of beauty
    Thou knewest once in thy lost star-home,
And know in fulfilling this oft irksome duty
    Swifter to glory thy steps will roam ! '

Silent the forest grew ; not a leaf trembled,
    Or flower whispered, syllable more,
While the fleet shadows dispersed and assembled
    Noiseless, in dances o'er the green floor.

Slowly the star-god turned sad from the sweetness
    Of blossoms recalling his lost home,

To seek in the strange world sense of completeness
    He dreamed he had missed in heaven's dome.


He came to a valley with pines straight growing
    Stern, stately, and grand to arching skies,
And felt in his soul that this all unknowing
    And peaceful spot grew dear in his eyes ;


So he rested and chose for his daily toil,
    Care and tending of trees and flowers,
Soft laying the seed in the fair fruitful soil,
    And watching it bud thro' changing hours ;


The blossoms springing reminded him faintly
    Of lost star fragrance, and joyed his heart,
While the stately trees so calm-browed and saintly
    Taught him to suffer, meek-eyed, his part :


And the people wondered at his sweet speaking,
    And fabled his home Arcadian land ;
And strove to inspire him with the wealth-seeking
    Hard spirit, they best could understand ;


But he turned from urging, with eyes uplifting
    Their calmness to blue sky overhead,
And murmured denial with sweetness, gifting
    Star-glow to commonest words he said :


Then they talked to him of their little story,
    Their wars—and battles—and soldiers' might—
How the German had won eternal glory,
    And Frenchman was beaten in the fight :

How their social science, and social measures
    Were leading the earth to perfect bliss;
While the sea was dredged for its buried treasures,
    And time was settled for mystic kiss

Of darkness and light, as the planets veiling
    In eclipse-shadow, their shining eyes
Came forth from the blackness, in beauty sailing
    With clear undimmed lustre thro' the skies :

They marvelled greatly that after relation
    Of tales of wonder and joy, or grief,
His calm brow nor smiled, nor showed elation,
    And always came answer low and brief :

' What does it matter?' he murmured slowly,
    Turned to his labour without a sigh
For the triumph-glory ; his mind too lowly,
    Recked not, they said, of aught grand or high.

They tried to excite his feelings, but vainly,
    With ' how do you like ?' ' would you prefer
But always he answered kindly but plainly ;
    ' The same 'tis to me ;' nor would defer

Duty of tendance for pleasure or gaining ;
    His soul rose above, to his lost star,
And he gazed in the moonlight to blue dome straining
    Tired eye with watching it beam afar.

Yet the people loved him, and sought untiring
    To draw his spirit within their grasp,

Not knowing that calm spirit was aspiring
　To heaven's rapture once his to clasp :

And they whispered his fairness had the glory
　Of moonlight blueness on starry night,
And recalled to their minds some saintly story
　Of angels descending thro' rays of light :

And the maidens half fearful, spoke all trembling
　Of glorious eyes (with vague alarm),
Which sought not their glances, only resembling
　Lily-kissed lakes in their moveless calm :

They knew not his brow bore echoes undying,
　Within its whiteness, of his lost star,
Which drowned all the voices of earthly sighing
　And drew his spirit into the far.

At last a youth-crowned and beauteous maiden,
　Cold to all lovers of earthly mould,
Wooed warmly but vainly by suitors love-laden,
　Chanced the star-god one day to behold :

His beauty and sadness pierced thro' the shielding
　Of loveless heart and high maiden pride,
And she worshipped him, suddenly up-yielding
　Spirit and soul to her new love-guide.

Alas for the maiden ! that she could never
　Let her heart answer a mortal voice ;
Seed only of star-love can blossom ever
　In his sad soul who became her choice !

K

She marvelled, and wept, that her fairness, striven
   For, as a jewel of untold price,
Touched him not at all to whom it was given ;
   He passed her unnoting—cold as ice.

There came a day once, when she watched him gazing
   Into the blueness, with tragic eyes ;
And her passion of words swept forth, upraising
   Pathos of sad love unto the skies :

' Oh why, my belovèd, with hopeless weeping
   Gazest thou into answerless skies ?
Let thy soul rest in the tender love-keeping
   Which speaks to thee clear in these brimming eyes.

' Turn not from pleasures most sweet in the tasting
   When shared with fair love, who blesses all ;
Ah, my belovèd one ! why art thou wasting
   Life hours but once safe within thy call?

' Look on me, maiden unmaidenly pleading
   For love treasure precious in my sight ;
Give not thy spirit to sleep and dream-leading,
   Turn from the shadow into life's light.

' Oh, my belovèd one ! have I not wondered,
   Watching thee ever with longing eyes,
What fearful doom life and spirit has sundered,
   Leaving earth empty, and hopeless skies.

' Canst thou not tell me, and find in the telling
   Peace for the anguish which saddens thee ?

Little thou knowest the deep love up-welling
   Over my heart, and constraining me

' Thus to pour forth on thy cold moveless hearing
   Passion of pity, and yearning too ;
What is the fate thou art trembling at nearing?
   Cannot pure love-light shine a way thro'?'

Softened and tender the star-god's blue eyes grew :
   Gravely he answered, 'Ah child, in vain
Sweetest of earth-loves to who sees the death thro',
   Happiness buds not for me again !

' I have known ideal rapture round-clasping
   Passionate fragrance of wings, and still
Sighed for a higher, diviner close-grasping
   Of what eluded my fervent will ;

' So all unknowing the bliss I was leaving,
   I floated down from yon distant star,
And reaching earth found that I had been grieving
   For shadows, which live not near or far :

' The voice which I heard 'mid the stars on-singing
   I vainly sought in all earthly bliss ;
It never was aught but my soul out-ringing,
   To greet the distant with poet kiss

' Of sweet impossible longing and yearning
   To grasp the substance, unknowing still
Even the shadow was but my soul turning
   Back on itself with wild eager will,

' Constrained by passionate heart of poet,
    A mystic chrism touching each thing
With a glory unspeakable, souls who know it
    Wear their hearts sore with striving to sing

' Its all impossible passion of glory ;
    Mortal words sink into soundless sighs,
And give no idea of the blissful story
    Poets see clear by their clear souls' eyes.

' Love that thou pleadest for, never was given
    Unto the true poet heart to feel ;
Too far his spirit from mortal aims riven
    For love to reign there—the man's life seal—

' No ; in his singing he sees but the many,
    Sings of their beauty, dreams of their love—
But never can choose as the only one, any
    To wear in his heart, and waft above :

' The love of the poet is for his singing ;
    The strife for the shadow holds it all ;
And voices of sweetness and earth-love ringing
    Like faintest echoes on his soul fall.

' Seek not, fair child, by thy sad tender pleading
    Sweetness like this which to bitter turns ;
Pity-feigned love bears but poisonous seeding—
    Hungry heart ever for fulness yearns,—

' And oft forgetting, in pain of that yearning
    Patience of waiting (the unloved's doom),

Crushes the buds of affection, swift spurning
    Promise of brightness in present gloom :

'Love is a star-crowned, steep ladder for climbing ;
    Possible—yes—but a weary toil !
Some creep up half-way ! while others subliming
    Souls to the combat, reck not the soil

' Of fair fingers bleeding with holding tightly
    Tremulous bending of earthly wood,
But bear heavy burdens with glad faces, lightly
    Suffering anguish for coming good ;

' Such souls undaunted find joy at the ending
    (Love's ladder reaches the highest star) ;
Yet those whose footsteps below them are wending
    Envy not glory seen from afar.

'Fair child, too tender and sweet for the mounting !
    Seek not the star, but earth's fragrant flow'rs :
Thou shalt find joy in their keeping and counting,
    And rose-crowned sing thro' life's passing hours :

' But if unheeding of sorrow, not counting
    Peril of heart, earth's joys cast away,
Thy soul firm chooses, and holds by, the mounting,
    Then, oh fair woman, there dawns a day

' When all the terror of darkness, and grasping
    Thorns to white breast with bitterest tears,
Shall be forgotten, and love crowned, round-clasping
    Beauty and rapture, be thine thro' all years !

' Thou wilt swift feel all the fragrance and sweetness
  Of my lost star-world, and comprehend
Emptiness of all mere earthly completeness
  To poet-soul who dreams of the end :

' Thy star with mine will be linked so divinely,
  Mortals may wonder if they be two,
As in the blueness enraptured, they finely
  Float on in glory the moonlight thro' !

' Plead not then, woman, for earth-love, swift turning
  Away from its object, seeking still
Ideal beauty and rapture, and yearning
  For more than mortal hearts can fill :

' Being the " distant," and far from thy clasping,
  Love seems eternal, and half divine,
But once the bloom near, and within thy grasping,
  Again beyond it new loves will shine:

' It is the fate of the artist and poet,
  And all whose high souls cling to a star,
Ever to dream of perfection, and know it,
  But see it beyond them down the far

' Of beauty impossible ! while their singing
  Strives to realise their fair dream,
But it soars above them with mighty winging,
  And words which describe it, lifeless seem.

' If thou would'st reach the fair glory at ending,
  Gather a wreath of noble deeds ;

' And unmoved, seeking not joy in thy wending,
　　Struggle on, heedless of earthly needs ;

' Nor rest that love, seeking still the ideal
　　On a poor blossom, or fading leaf ;
Bitter the wak'ning to find but the real !
　　Earth-love illusion ever is brief :

' Think of the star-worlds, dream but of their beauty ;
　　Into their rapture plunge thee deep ;
And every step of mere earthly duty
　　Will be to their bliss a full soul-leap.'—

Hushed lay the world while the star-god and poet
　　Spoke from his soul the whole earth's strong need ;
Then a whisper arose ; ' We all feel it, and know it—
　　And weep it forth, but man will not heed ;

' He passes us by with scornful exclaiming ;
　　" I alone speak, all the rest are mute ; "
And in his haughtiness gives us a naming
　　And crushes our beauty with absolute

' Hardness of planting, and taming, unknowing
　　The secret law which our being guides ;
So he turns the stream to the ocean flowing
　　With musical murmuring green sides,

' Into a channel smoke-grimed with his shipping ;
　　Bearing, instead of its swans and blooms
And jewelled butterflies sunnily skipping,
　　Poisonous drugs to his cities' glooms.

' 'Tis but a poet, slow-growing for ages,
    From heaven-rays caught in common mould,
Who knows us, and rippling thro' his sweet pages
    Glimpses of beauty shine forth untold ;

' He clearly sees (but alas for his vision !)
    Words fail, and shrink into soundless tone ;
And the hard world recks not the true prevision
    Which its poor poet has made his own ;

' But calls him "dreamer," and places with scorning
    Pebbles of custom to block his way ;
And then, when he stumbles, instead of mourning,
    And helping him softly, what does it say ;

' But, " Ah thou prophet ! with all thy fair teachings,
    Canst thou not tread a path to us clear ?
What is the good of thy mighty star-reachings
    If thou must stumble and fall down here ? "

' So the poor bruised cast-down soul of the poet
    Comes back to nature, to mourn alone
With the sweetness and beauty, who well know it
    And comfort it softly with each tone :

' And we pour such wonderful dreams of blisses
    (Germs of possible budding life)
Into his mind, with the fragrant kisses
    Borne to his brow by the cool wind's strife ;

' That he, all forgetful of former falling,
    Struggles again thro' his hard life-round,

And hears 'mid earth's clanging the angels calling
  With blissful murmur of waving sound.'—

Sank into stillness the mystical singing ;
  Faintly the pale stars shone overhead ;
Plashing of ocean heard distantly ringing
  Greeted the rising moon, rosy red,

Drifting the blue thro' ; in eagerness veiling
  Bright face 'neath snow of breeze-driven cloud,
But swift in splendour and majesty sailing
  Thro' the wide arch to her beauty bowed :

Then a great calmness sank down on the maiden,
  Law of repression had found her heart,
Rhythm of beauty, whose form passion-laden
  Souls cannot grasp ; and she did depart,

With sad eyes love-yearning, back-turned no longer
  To him watching calm the distant blue ;
For her life had grown in that murmur stronger
  And heaven's beauty had pierced it thro'.

Never again would the earth-love up-springing
  Turn her soul from the possible star ;
No : her soaring spirit thro' rapture winging
  Would rest not until it reached the ' far.'—

So the years rolled on, and the people striving
  No more to draw him within their ken,
The star-god passed calmly his life, deriving
  All pleasure from nature, far from men :

And they called him 'dreamer,' and muttered slowly
  He came of a harmless, helpless race,
With no mind, or soul, and with heart too lowly
  To answer the beauty of his face:

And he poured forth rapturous, deathless singing,
  As inspiration flooded his mind;
But ever the fragrance of angel-winging
  Whispered of glory still left behind:

While his songs (the true artist's soul out-flowing)
  More suggested than fully exprest;
So that those who read them felt half unknowing
  A dim recalling of what was best

In all their lives, and a possible glory
  Springing thence into the highest sky,
And marvelled heart-pierced on the poet's story,
  And felt his power, and wondered why;

For his words sped forth thro' the dark world name-
  (No name had the one who gave them birth); [less
His poems struck home, nor were rendered aimless
  By lack in the man of human worth:

And the girl who loved him, her love down-casting
  In self-abasement, gathered a crown
Of noble, pure actions, more sweet and lasting
  Than passion's rapture, or earth's renown :—

And she faded gently, and in the gloaming
  Of one fair and silent summer-day,

Her soaring spirit, set free from its roaming
　On weary earth, took its joyous way,

And swift thro' the blueness of ether winging
　Pierced the sky-dome, a radiant star
Whose voice the poet could hear 'mid the singing
　Of mystic sphere-music, and afar

Gazing calm-eyed saw it rapturous sailing
　Over his life with a guiding eye ;
And he sighed, ' Ah love, thou hast true unveiling,
　And knowest star-beauty in the fair sky ;

' Now I can love thee, my ideal glory !
　Star I have lost, but shall find once more ;
Bless me, oh dream-love ! and whisper my story
　In thro' the rapture of heaven's door,

' That I may be freed from this earth, which drew me
　By moonlight beauty to her cold breast ;
And struck back the rapture which rippled thro' me,
　And fragrance of loving harsh represt ;

' That I may once more feel wings strongly flutter
　In passionate, boundless, eager flight,
And taste all the blisses words cannot utter,
　Revealed to me in thy tender light !

' Ah, my belovèd ! if far-distant gazing
　Floods my spirit with beauty and love,
What will the end be when clearly upraising
　Pinions I float on, a star above ?

' Thine was the voice whose unspeakable sweetness
   Drew me the blueness and moonlight thro';
Now I see clear, not but dream of completeness ;
   For, oh belovèd, it dwells in you !

' It was the germ of the possible mounting
   Hid in thy soul, whose echo in mine
Led me from blisses of rapture, not counting
   Star-glow without thee, beauty divine.'—

He turned, with the calm-eyed patience, which never
   Left his white brow, to his work and rest,
But a prayer-longing was wafted ever
   Across the distance to her star's breast ;

As each night fell down with its dimness, shading
   Long-parted hearts into love once more
By mystic yearning for oneness unfading,
   Daylight sees not on its golden floor,

Nor heeds the trueness, that unity presses
   Unlovely fragments in lovely whole,
And all humanity in its recesses
   Bears only the impress of one soul :

Oh night ! the revealer of hidden feelings,
   Of choked back terror and deathless love,
Filling our souls with the gracious healings
   Heaven holds in mercy clouds above ;

And pours down softly in sleep to the mourner—
   Rest and calm to the weariest one—

And the higher blessing to souls forlorner
   Of death-releasing, while sleeps the sun ;

How oft in thy silence of coldness, breathless
   With yearning eyes ever upward turned,
Did the star-god gaze, while with brightness deathless
   Her star above in the blueness burned :

Till one night he felt longing, half unknowing
   Floating away into deepest rest,
And his spirit knew star-rapture in-flowing
   Thro' all the calmness of his sad breast ;

And he mused with that love, whose strength divineth
   Thought of the loved one, without a word ;
' My star-love's prayers, as for me she pineth
   Have floated thro' space, and now are heard ;

' And the golden fragrance of doors whose clasping
   Binds the zone of the fair angel band
Has opened, and thro' all the darkness gasping
   My soaring brothers have sought this land :

' They come, oh the bright ones ! down ether winging,
   To carry me back to my lost star ;
The soft moonlight quivers to hear their singing,
   And wooes them to rest in it afar ;

' But onward the passionate white wings flutter ;
   Oh rapture of fragrant flight untold !
My soul longs with yearnings I cannot utter
   To feel once more the close snowy fold,

'And soar, and soar with the ever unchanging
　　Joy of the winging from star to star,
With no earth-tiring, no death, and no changing,
　　But ever fresh beauty in the far.'

And the white-winged, star-crowned angel creatures
　　Floated down swiftly, and touched his home
With their glowing pinions and fire-strong features,
　　Till it gleamed with glory like their own ;

While the pure flame (spurning the earthly veiling
　　Which hid the star-god's beauty divine)
Rose, round him flowing and o'er him sailing
　　Until he shone with the mystic shine

Of moonlight glory and rapture's revealing,
　　Sought for in vain, but now in his grasp ;
For the strength of conquering love bore healing,
　　And might of blessing within its clasp :

So the star-god, with beauty undimmed by the passing
　　A yearning poet-life on earth,
And tasting the depths of her sad alas —ing,
　　And learning how faint, and little worth

The answerless nature within our longings
　　Must be to the soul who cannot soar,
Nor hear above, the tuned answering songings
　　Which the stars chant on for evermore :

And having with deathless singing, the human
　　Taught to question its guiding soul,

And let star-rapture and beauty flow thro' man
  Whispering dreams of his far-off goal ;

Rose swift above, thro' the moonlight, aspiring
  Again to reach his dreamings fulfilled ;
And his eager pinions, snow-spread untiring,
  Bore him thro' blueness where he willed :

So he soared to his star-home, once more glowing
  With joy of realised poet's dream ;
And felt in his soul the rapture all-knowing
  Of conquered self, in its silver beam ;

And the love who waited with prayers falling
  Like burning tears on the golden gate,
While her song was ever an upward calling,
  A passion of music, sad as fate,

For her star-god left lonely on earth, bearing
  With calm poet-heart his dream's decline,
And raising blue eyes to the blueness, caring
  Alone for the beauty of her shine ;

Now felt his presence with mighty quivering ;
  And sped cloud-speed to his star's embrace,
And he clasped her close—his great delivering
  Shedding new beauty o'er his god-face ;

And fast united, they sail on for ever,
  Two stars in one with a double light,
Whose glory, thro' darkness expiring never
  Whispers of rapture and star-love bright.

Next morn when the people arose from sleeping,
    The star-god's dwelling in ruins lay :
And they gazed, and wondered, and some half weeping
    Cleared the poor blackened fragments away,

And sought with tenderness unavailing
    To find the poet, who was not there,
But far above their blind labours was sailing
    In rapture of star-bloom thro' the air :

And they said at last (their voices low-toning),
    ' The fate of dreamers is ever thus ;
No shadow of earth care, or human groaning,
    Brought his beauty nigh unto us ;

' And now behold ! in the darkness unknowing,
    When slumber soft on our spirits fell,
And rest from anguish o'er all men was flowing,
    His soul was taken ; nor left to tell

' The tale of his passing one human creature ;
    Alone did he live, and so did he die :
And of his beauty no one earthly feature
    Remains, in peace 'neath the grass to lie.'

And their men of science, with sharp eyes casting
    Spying glances far into the blue,
With their small minds seeking the everlasting
    Glory of heaven soft peeping thro',

Found one day at last, with great acclamation,
    A new and wonderful double star ;

And proclaimed the marvel with exaltation
  That science sublime could reach so far ;

And they gave it an earthly name, and weighed it,
  And sought its radiance to describe
By telling of metals which they had made it
  Reveal to them burning, thro' glass bribe !

And the people talked of advance, and wonder
  Of knowledge, their boundless souls could win ;
How their science tore the heavens asunder,
  And forced a way for their spirits in,

Till nothing remained of fear or mystery
  But their eyes had pierced its hidden fold,
And written out clear the planet's history—
  And measured the length of the sun's gold :—

And they thought no more of the star-god poet
  Whose song to listening souls spoke clear ;
They had had revealing, and did not know it :
  Ah fate of all inspiration here !

We nations see but shadow casting
  Its weight on the earth, nor look above
Where the substance in beauty everlasting
  Reigns and blossoms and waits for our love ;

And we pride ourselves on our minds upraising
  Boundless pyramids over the sand
Of our life ocean ; and stifle with praising
  The work of a feeble human hand ;

L

Nor heed the truth which to future seeking
   Will be revealed, that our mighty tombs
Are merely the emptiness, broadly speaking,
   Of soul which lost itself in their glooms !

## LOST HAPPINESS.

My darling, oh my darling, now the joyous spring
  is here,
    Wilt thou come back to me smiling,
    With thy low sweet voice beguiling
       All my fear
Into depths of merely loving, while I gaze down
  eyes of blue
In a tender mist of tear-drops all their beauty shining thro'?
Oh my own, my twilight love-dream, with thy breeze-
  stirred fragrant hair
Floating shadow-like around thee, oh thou sweetest
  and most fair!
  Oh my darling, come anear me, let thy little fingers
    twine
       Into mine,
And resting there securely, let me hear thee whisper
  low;
'I will kiss thee in the twilight, and the daylight
  shall not know.'

  Then, belovèd, I will crown thee with the purple
    violet,
  Pale primroses and narcissus, and the sweetest
    blooms that yet
In the fairness of our mother earth the blessèd spring
  has set—

I will fling their sweetness o'er thee, oh my own,
    my little one,
And thou shalt backward toss me
        Only one,
Just one lily for an emblem of thy youth and purity,
And my heart shall wear that blossom thro' the dim
    eternity.—

Oh my darling, now the spring-time with each happy
    singing-bird
      Has come forth from winter's veiling,
      And now suns are brightly sailing,
        And are heard
      All the myriad sounds, so gaily
      Flooding all the hard world daily
Till the poet's soul springs upward, and his brows can
    reach the stars,
And his bounding heart re-echoes all the shining dim
    afars,
Where the dreams of ancient singers are hid deep be-
    yond the ken
Of the merely earthly-seeking, groping humanness of
    men.—

      Wilt thou not come to me, sweetest?
        See ! I open wide my arms,
      And my heart, with bitter longings
          For the calms
      Which have fled with footsteps fleetest
          'Mid alarms
That they never will return, and my vain and empty
    songings

Are but beatings of despair against the iron wall of
    fate,
      Which is higher than our reaching—
      And lies far beyond our preaching—
And the knowledge of whose mystery will dawn not
    till too late !


      Oh my sweetest, let a whisper
        Fall upon my waiting heart
      Till it drown the babbling lisper
          That apart
Seeks to strike us with the clangour of her wailing dis-
    cord notes ;
Let the sighing breeze re-echo, as around my brow it
    floats,
      The veiled sweetness of thy singing
      Thro' the stilly twilight ringing,
And not merely all the sadness which so agonised and
    low
Flies out dimly thro' the darkness, which is all my soul
    can know
      Of the land where thou art dwelling,
      Since that time so long ago—
        Since that spring-tide when we parted
          Broken-hearted
          In the glow
      Of the blossomy bright weather,
      When the breezes swept the heather
        Swift or slow
      As by sun or cloud on-driven
        They did go ;

While the shadows softly lengthened
 Till the veil of heaven was riven,
  And forgiven
All the earthliness dropt from us, and our souls sprang
 upward strengthened,
 And we paced the earth together
 As if God dwelt everywhere !
  Oh how fair
 Blooms that evening's wild revealing,
 And the blissfulness of feeling,
As our fingers clung together, and my eyes gazed deep
 in thine,
 That the love my heart held dearer
 Than itself, but drew it nearer
To the beauty of the universe — the one pervading
 soul !
 For all the myriad glories,
 And the high heroic stories—
 Music's rapture—art's proud dreaming—
 Fairness ever brighter gleaming
In the eyes of the beloved one, are but fragments of
 the whole—
Scattered star-beams of the beauty gath'ring strength
 as onward rolls
The unceasing subtle-changing earth, between her
 guiding poles.—

 Ah my sweetest, all the glory
  Faded swifter than it came !
 And it seems some olden story,
  Or dim legend with no name ;

Yet it woke the soul within me, springing up with
    sudden flame,
        And I knew I was a poet,
        And I felt that thou didst know it,
And the joy that knowledge gave was far dearer than
    the fame
        Which the years have showered o'er me,
        And all men have laid before me,
            With no blame
      For the weakness in my singing—
      For the half-tones ever ringing
        With one name ;
      And the minor sounding ever
    'Mid the music's glad acclaim ;
      For, oh dearest, I can never
    While life lasts, forget those eyes,
And they whisper 'mid life's tumult of the calmness
    in the skies ;
And they draw me ever upward to the rapture of
    the stars
Till my soul forgets her singing, and but murmurs
    of afars,—
And again the heavens open and reveal their bliss
    to me ;
Oh my darling, earth is heaven when my spirit
    reaches thee !

But alas ! the vision passes, as reality has passed
And my spirit, tasting heaven, to the cold earth back
    is cast :
      Oh my darling, I am lonely,
      And this spring-tide whispers only

'Mid its music, and its blossom, and its happy sweet
    bird-songs,
Of that other blither spring-tide whose fair glory could
    not last ;
And the throngs
Of wild thoughts and bitter longings flood my yearning
    soul in vain,
For the beauty of that spring-tide can for me ne'er
    bloom again.

But oh sweetest, thro' the twilight
  Bid the fluttering angel-wings
Sweep down softly ere the star-light
  Its wild mystic chant out-rings
All the earth to flood with glory,
While the mountains bare and hoary
  Lie reflected in the ocean
  Surging with a wild emotion
And a strife to reach the fairness shadowed in its
  depths, and sings
  To the shore with fainter plashing
  Of its waves, for ever clashing
Will to will against the power
Given the earth to hold her dower
  Of fair cities and green trees—
    On my knees
I beseech a sign or token
That our love-vow is not broken;
Oh my one love, give me answer down the sighing of
  the breeze ;
Let thy spirit for one instant swiftly from the heaven fly
To thy earthly lover, winging thro' fair blueness of the
  sky.—

Sweetheart, 'tis the happy spring-time ;
    Crocus flames are springing bright,
Golden, purple, snowy chaliced
        In the light
Which the waking sun doth quiver
    O'er the throbbing, pulsing earth-veil—
Here with snowdrops and narcissus
        Fair and pale,
    There with purple glory turning
        Violets into lips to kiss us,
        And now burning
Into daffodils whose beauty, golden, dewy-eyed and
    tall,
Seems like shadows of the star-lights gleaming clear
    thro' heaven's wall ;
Ah my sweetest, like a love-crown thy flower-face
    peeps thro' them all !
        While the river
    Flowing with a murm'ring sound,
        And a rime
    From the dimness of the mountains
        Where its youth first sprang to light,
    'Mid the snowy air-kissed fountains
        And the stately rocks high-palaced
        Of the height—
Whispers to my yearning fancy but thy name with
    myriad tone,
Echoing my craving sighing for one glimpse of thee,
    my own !—


    But the breeze sighs on unheeding
        With its dreary monotone,

And the passion of my pleading
  Falls alone
Down the silent twilight throbbing
With its waking stars to life,
    While the strife
To catch echoes from the regions
Which are hidden from our knowing,
    But felt drearily,
      And wearily,
When dear ones to them going,
Flood their dimness with the legions
  Of their passing spirits, robbing
Earth of all its pleasant fairness, and the spring-tide
    of its youth ;
For the sweetest is the fleetest to depart, and this sad
    truth
Ever rings amid the music of the highest earthly bliss ;
'What is lost is ever dearest,' and no present love's
    warm kiss
Can ever fill our spirits like the lost love that we miss !

## THISTLE-BLOSSOM.

No legend this of fabled ancient time,
    Lost in the mist of proofless ignorance,
Tho' bearing in its bosom deeds sublime
    The blossoms of world's youth, intolerance—
Intolerance of meanness—cowardice,
    Fair speech and treach'rous action, which lead still
To deeper hells than churchmen frame I wis,
    Or bigots hold with hard relentless will
    To crush the life of freedom in our souls, and kill

The possibility so humanly
    Soft springing with world spring, that crocus flame
Lights up with splendour glowing all that we
    Find echoing in our souls and speaks the name
Of happiness made perfect thro' the strife—
    Of hope-bells ringing pæans for the fight,
In snowdrop glimm'ring 'mid its peaceful life,
    Or violet springing purple-crowned to light,
    And all the young earth's beauty breaking on our
        sight !

Her loveliness, o'erpowering our soul
    With mighty rapture 'mid the joyous spring,
Doth it not murmur of the yearned-for goal
    With every bloom or flutter of bird-wing?

Doth not the streamlet wand'ring whispering
  ' I, happy, seek full happiness where I
Feel dimly my fate lies, and onward sing,
  Clear gazing upward to the gleaming sky ;
Thro' flowers I go, thro' wedding-bells that ring,
Thro' forests' gloomy darkness, lonely, yet I sing ; '

And like that brooklet, half unknowing still
  The meaning of its song, yet singing clear
Because its full heart and its chainless rill
  Make music of the present and the near ;
So I from throbbing life, in this our time
  Catch melodies familiar yet more sweet
Than past romances, and my simple rime
  Flows from my full heart, kindred hearts to greet
  And guide to higher grander climbing weary feet.

The poet sees in common daily life,
  In earth's most usual landmarks, loveliness—
Can trace in bud and flower the endless strife,
  The quivering upward, and the dreams that press
The rose's glowing heart to open fair
  Its sweetness to the sun ; while the slight lark,
Tho' leaving love on earth, still seeks the air
  With dawn's first blush, and only in life's dark
  Can quench with human blessings inspiration's
    spark.

And as tho' colourless the beam of light
  May pass the crystal medium on its way,
Nor think the earthly goblet has the might
  To change the whiteness of its snowy ray ;

Yet look and see in countless glowing tints
  The ray appears transmuted—move the glass—
The glory fades, for broken are the hints
  Which earth may give of heaven, and alas
  They need the poet's soul all pure thro' which to
    pass !

And is mine so ?  I know not, nor can guess,
  For there are depths unsounded and unknown
In every human soul, which can express
  Sweet music or the harshest discord tone :
Oh life ! oh fate ! be merciful to me,
  Give me the poet's soul, and make me strong ;
I love the heights, I love the purity
  Of calm endurance, echoing not wrong,
  But weaving beauty-dreams, in actions all life
    long.—

Oh stars, send down your brightness on my heart,
  Drop your eternal calmness down on me ;
Let me, oh watchers, link my human part
  Of helpless longing, to sublimity
In gazing at your light !—like Dante, I
  Would wish to end each song with that word
    ' star '—
The type of highest possibility—
  A whisper of the lowly to the far—
  A yearning for the calmness of the ruler Star !

## PART I.

A BARE stretch of grey moorland, toned and touched,
When sunlight glittered, with a gleam of gold
From yellow waving corn.   The tender heart
Hid in the bareness struggled to express
Its dreams of beauty in the purple glow
Of heather bloom, like rosy blush of love
Struggling thro' calmness of a hard borne life—
Behind the moorland rose serene dark pines,
Raising their sombre heads upright and bare—
No tendril ivy clung, no blossom drooped
Round the straight stems, and yet the sun had given
A deeper colour, an intenser glow,
To those bare stems, than any blossoms frail,
Which cling in summer, but when dark days dawn
And winds are howling in their mad career
Shrink into dust and nothingness, nor leave
A pledge of loving to the desolate.—
The deep pines' wavelike murmur dashing on
(With ceaseless whisper of unuttered dreams),
The blue air's shimm'ring shore, spoke clear to one
Who dwelt beneath their shadow ; and his soul,
To art full-consecrate, took deeper draughts
Of truth and beauty 'mid the solitude ;
No loneliness to one who could express
In colouring of Nature all the thoughts,
The dreams, the aims, the longings, of the trees,
And read the voice of waving in the grass,
Or dewdrop in the bloom, or falling leaf,
Or humble moss with glowing scarlet seal

To guard the treasure of its fairy cup
From prying ant, or buzzing summer fly :
He knew, perhaps, the treasure out of sight
Might well seem precious, and its rarity
The tiny moss held sacred, tho' alas,
Mere emptiness appeared to common eyes
Beneath the mystic chrism of the cup.
He painted thus so humanly, each spray,
Each leaf, bore its own impress and made clear
A character full written, and each bloom
Sang its own meaning from the canvas, plain,
And spoke to poets—artists—for all time
Expressing clear the boundless humanness
Seen not alone in man but each still life
Same spirit, with but different shades of growth—
Beneath the pines he dwelt, and pondered deep
On all the systems which humanity
Had slow invented, to bind down its soul
To usual common living, that its wings
Might never soar above the firm hard ground
Of ' I believe ;' ''tis God's will,' and so forth,
The ever uttered answers, given swift
With sombre brow, and terror-stricken eye
To question of the free.   'Tis not ' I know ;'
But, ' I believe ;' they dare not seek to know ;
Alas that this should be ! alas ! alas !
What hope of happiness when all our life
Is founded on a fancy, not a truth ?
For truth until discovered to be such,
And not alone discovered, but made clear
With demonstration far beyond dispute,
May well be fable ; and our manliness,

Our hero-strifes, our dream-thoughts, and our aims
Are wrecked alike on this one rock of ' fear '—
Fear to look into darkness—fear to find
We know not what dim horror in the dusk.
Not so my artist : the calm standing pines
And bracing moorland strengthenèd his soul,
And, eagle-like, he dared to face the sun,
Or, fearless, mole-like burrow in the dark
Of the world's by-ways, seeking everywhere
A truth which he dare hold to light the earth
With touch of faith and reason, budding fair,
And bearing blossoms of heroic deeds
To strew the rugged pathway to the stars.
He listened while his kindred the dark pines,
With surging motion, murmured doubtfully :

' Wilt thou never, never learn it, never  learn it, doubt
     or spurn it ?
   Is our melancholy sighing all in vain ?
All the winds thro' us are rushing, flowers crushing,
     song-birds hushing,
   Is there none to hear our crying and our pain ?

' Now triumphantly we spurn them, fling them from us,
     backward turn them,
   And our voices sink a moment into rest ;
But these winds are so persisting, there is no hope of
     resisting,
   For they fly to us from north, south, east and west !

' We have dim  mysterious feelings of some future
     gracious healings
   Which will come some day if only we are heard ;

But mankind pass on unheeding of our rapture or
our needing,
And alas ! in vain each sigh or wailing word.


' Oh true artist, swiftly listen, rise and hear while dew-
drops glisten ;
Watch the dawning and the waning of each star ;
Ope thy fair soul's golden portal, let her hear the
song immortal,
Send thy fearless spirit seeking down the far.


'Know the deep sky's gleaming blueness, and the
magic air-wave's thro'ness
Are but shadows of the possible in life ;
While a flash of inspiration, bearing godlike wise
elation,
Speak the constant stars on-shining o'er the strife ;


'While the highest dream of any, ever hidden from the
many,
All the human on earth seeking highest flight,
That most glorious dream of one god, springs itself
from the low world-sod,
'Tis humanity grown perfect in the light !'

So did my artist open all his soul
To the low sighing of the universe ;
His longings and his searchings did outflow
In torrent of full song which thus expressed
Itself in music, to the monotone
Of swinging pine-boughs, and of heather stirred
By wayward breeze which swept down from the
hills :—

M

'Thy sun upon me,
  Thy winds around,
No creeds shall bind me
  Till thou art found !
Thy dewdrops glisten,
  Thy flowers smile ;
My soul must listen
  Yet for awhile ;
Sweet Nature's voices
  Speak to me clear,
Each thing rejoices,
  Why should I fear ?
Thou art my father,
  I am thine own,
Would I then rather
  Be left alone ?
No ; for the beauty
  None can express
Of thy smile on me
  Sweet to excess—
Of thy voice to me
  'Mid starry night,
In the winds round me
  Murmuring light ;
Tho' the full union
  Here has no place,
Spiritual communion
  Shadows thy grace :
All things of beauty
  Typify thee,
Making hard duty
  Love-service free !

O'er the snow-mountain
  My soul doth climb,
By scented fountain,
  'Neath fragrant lime,
'Mid forests ancient—
  In every place
My spirit patient
  Sees clear thy face.
Ah god ! love ! brother !
  Come to me now !
Where is another
  Lovely as thou ?
I cannot tell them
  How I know thee ;
I cannot make them
  Happy and free ;
They will not know thee,
  Or comprehend
What thou art to me ;
  Nearer than friend—
Closer than brother—
  Dearer than all—
I need no other,
  Thou art them all !
So, they reproach me,
  Make my soul grieve ;
But god, thou know'st me,
  That I believe ;
Help me, oh fair lord,
  And my soul save
When it sinks toward
  Despair's deep wave ;

Send then thy love-smile
    Straight to my heart,
Keep me thine own, while
    We are apart :
Here in the dim light
    Of our dark star,
Glimpses of thy light
    Gleam from afar :
'Mid tinsel glories
    Of passing creeds,
In the old stories
    Of noble deeds ;
'Mid the grief-languish
    Of the death room,
Softening its anguish
    Lightening its gloom ;
Thro' all a sunbeam,
    From thee doth fall,
As the fair gold-gleam
    Sanctifies all
Trouble and danger,
    Anguish and toil—
Life with the stranger
    On foreign soil—
Have no more power
    O'er the man's soul
Now his sought dower
    Gleams from the goal :
So in my seeking,
    Falsehood and crime
Melted, repeating
    Lies to all time ;

But still I found thee
   Shining thro' all,
Like a fair jewel
   Hid 'neath a pall.
Custom's chains bound me
   Far from the light ;
Error's waves drowned me
   In deepest night ;
Then in my sorrow
   I turned to thee ;
Soon dawned the morrow
   Joyous and free :
Shadows have left me,
   Doubts are no more,
Truth's unveiled radiance
   Dawns from the shore ;
Ghosts of creeds vanished
   Melt in the light
Of true life, banished
   From my rapt sight ;
For now morn breaketh
   O'er death's dark night,
My soul awaketh,
   And it is light ! '

So sang he, and in singing swept away
The mist of ignorance which ever clings
Unto the soul of weak humanity,
Until the unveiled art reveals herself
To chosen hearts, and touches them with fire,
And they see clearly ; tho' their words express
Not half the meaning and the rarity

Of beauty that they know—his artist mind,
Swept like a harp by Nature's witching hand,
Gave forth a sweetness inexpressible,
And sent the true tone from its inmost depths
Which we call inspiration ;—so he knew
The meaning of the pine-song, that the sky
With broad blue arch o'ersheltering our life,
And bearing calmness of eternal stars,
Was but the height of possibility
Within our human reach, with piercing flash
Of inspiration lighting up its depths
To softer radiance and intenser might,
And showing far beneath the frippery
Of tinsel creeds and dogmas harsh down-pressed
On weary brows to crush them, and cast down
In dust of earth the yearning for the stars,
A statue calm, sublime—the human god—
The god of humanness—the highest form—
The type of human possibility !—
Who can imagine that which lies beyond
His nature and his mind ?   Impossible
The strife to grasp a phantom which eludes
With Proteus change our seeking ; if indeed
The God we hear of is beyond our ken,
Why seek to comprehend the mystery,
The hopelessness, of faith in what dwells far
Beyond the grasp of longest human arms—
Above the height of highest human souls—
Below the depth of broadest human hearts—
'Tis vanity and sloth which urge men still
To bow their reason to the priestly thrall
Which speaks of comprehension as a sin,

And seeking, as a crime most worthy hell ;
And lulls men to dull slumber on the earth
With dreams of God, far over human power
To reach or equal—leave him, brothers, there ;
A solitary form—an emptiness—
A mere negation, feelingless and cold—
A rock where warm hearts beat themselves in vain
To deeper deaths—but brothers, hear the truth
My artist found, and finding, laid his life
Before the treasure as an offering,
A lamp to shine for ever, and guide men
Far from the phantoms to reality—
Deep thought he 'mid the silence of the wood ;
No rest or sleep his seeking spirit knew ;
He watched the rising of th' eternal stars—
He marked their waning when the sun arose—
He listened to the breathing loveliness
Of moss and fern—to rapture of green leaves—
To tender longings of the budding flowers—
To every twitter of the singing birds—
To all sound and all silence :—when night fell
And breezes whispered thro' the swinging bough
His soul sought in rapt music mysteries
Which even Nature knows not, and he played
With merest shadow of caressing sound
That wondrous moonlight poem—how it flowed—
A dream of harmony ; a chime of stars ;
A vision of the wild moon-driven clouds :—
First slowly dropping weary solemn tones
A soul in shadow of earth's littleness,
With gleams of heaven's beauty streaming thro,'
A whisper from the god humanity

Fast prisoned in its depths :—low, dim at first
The whisper comes, as overarching trees
Catch the fair moonbeams from the poet's brow
Sad waiting for their crown, but gath'ring bright
With every gliding note, until at last
The forest passes, and full moonlight glow
Rises in glory, and the blue above
Intenser burns, and earth is out of sight,
But snowy angels fill the distant air
And drop the gladness of their melodies
Into the waiting lonely poet-heart,
And so the songs we marvel at have birth :—
The rapture passes as the strife had passed,
And now the wonders of the night lie bare ;
The white wild clouds fly raving thro' the sky :
The stars are hidden ; the moon veils her face ;
And swift alternate lights and shades flit by ;
The blueness rocks—the angel bands sweep on ;
A murmur greeting rises from the earth
(Still out of sight to the rapt poet's mind),
And mingles with the star-song, till at last
United is humanity with God !
Nay, rather God has crowned humanity
With precious jewel of its own great heart !—
Thus did that music poem clear express
Its meaning to the poet ; when I say
An artist, poet, or musician,
I mean one bearing on his fair life-shield
A shadow of true art, not separate :
('Tis but our littleness which cuts away
A portion from its home, and with false pride,
That child of ignorance, and loud high voice

Declares it whole—) all art is one alone,
Seen but from diff'rent views, at diff'rent times,
And speaking myriad-voiced to gazing souls.
One even as his fingers kissed the keys,
And wooed their sweetness in low undertone
To sing to him of angels with the grail,
And white clouds floating thro' the bare blue heav'n,
And Lohengrin in quest of holiness —
(It was a blissful dream half-realised
Of his own search for pure humanity ;
And struck straight from the poet heart who sang
Into his own with mighty echoing) ;
He turned his rapt face to the loveliness
Of harmony without, beneath the moon,
And knew a thrill swift quivering adown
His spirit to its depths—a ripple sweep
Of passionate delight which seemed to breathe,
And yet half trembled in its blissfulness ;
For lo! the Nature had sprung into life
With highest glory! and stood typified
In a fair maiden, standing goddess-wise
With stedfast eyes upturned, hair backward thrown,
And white hands claspèd in an ecstasy:
Was it the magic of the holy grail?
Had Elsa come to life? or had his dreams
Thus shaped their own fair fruition at last ?
Well might he wonder, for a sweeter dream
Sure never gladdened a true artist soul.—
Serene she stood; the patient stars had given
A crown of calmness to the broad white brow,
And azure blueness with wind-driven sighs
Of floating cloud-dreams whispered in her eyes ;

Her dark hair threaded with a gleam of gold
Fell rippling down the night, and made it glow
With subtle perfume of the nature pure
Deep dwelling in her soul.   His fingers strayed
Unknowing o'er the keys, and warbled forth
The passionate full rapture Lohengrin
Found in his bridal song, and then slow drew
The wailing, melting excess of sad love
Which follows rapture in that master-mind
Who sweeps the whole chord of humanity,
And speaks in tones so true, that half the world
Feign him a madman—inspiration's fate
In this earth ever is to be called mad !
Mad as the angels !   Christ would be called mad
Now, as of old ; let one but try His words
Writ into actions, all the world lifts eyes
Of scornful pity on the blasphemer
Of long-established custom, and stones him
With social pebbles of sharp stinging slights,
And poison-drop in sweet of his life's cup ;
In hope, perchance, he dash the goblet down,
And die despairing !—As the last notes passed,
And silence like a presence downward fell,
He dared to near the vision, to make clear
His dazzled eyes that she indeed stood there,
A portion of the sleeping loveliness,
The pine-wood's tender soul.   The moonlight caught
With soft caress her downward streaming hair,
As half surprised, half rapturous, she turned
To wonder why the sweetness of the tone
Had died away, and left—my artist there !
They stood with eyes straight gazing each at each,

A rapture and a passion in each soul
Ne'er felt before, and inexpressible,
But deathless in its might.   Oh glowing souls,
Why must the torture of a hopeless love
Blaze in your depths? a glory, yet a curse !
Why must a passion reaching unto heav'n
In its wide grasping boundlessness, shrink back
To a mere fading earthly dream ?   Oh love !
Oh piercing sweetness, passing bitterly
To dust and ashes !   Oh the serpent trail
Amidst the flowers, crushing out their life,
Stifling their fragrance, making pale their hues
In yearning for the inexpressible,
Impossible of love !   Immortal love,
The deathless passion of exalted souls,
How can the dull earth satisfy thy needs?
We think (poor fools) with a most childish wish,
Of each new treasure our hearts hunger for,
' Oh if it were but mine, my life would be
A Paradise !'   No longing dwells beyond
(So in our blindness dream we) the dear 'now
Of coveted possession ; but alas
The jewel ours, how different its ray !
How faded, dim, and earthly doth it shine
Upon our earthly finger, tho' it gleamed
Star-like while out of reach !   'Tis ever so—
Love, fame, and glory blossom valueless
When woven in our crown ; 'tis when above
Our feeble grasp they hang, we hold them dear,
And strive to pluck, and die ; or living, find
Attainment vain, content an empty dream.—
He strove to speak, and holding forth his hand,

Hers, like a white dove, fluttered to his clasp
With utter trustfulness of innocence ;
And so these children of humanity,
Each with a gospel budding silently
In fragrant youthful heart, stood drinking deep
The poison rapture of a deathless love.—
'Whence come you? from the clouds or music-land?'
At last he uttered ; and the speaking dream
Made answer, rippling with a sweet low laugh,
'No ; the enchanted forest drew me forth
With mystic singing of the moonlight boughs ;
My home (a cold one) lies beyond the bound
Of its fair leafage, over the wide heath,
Upon the distant blue of yonder hill ;
And you,'—she paused, as memory's swift flash
Recalled the blissful tones of Lohengrin,
And marvelled if a question broke the dream,
And cast him into shadow-land again :
'I dwell beneath the pine-boughs,' answered he,
'And paint fair Nature as she speaks to me ;
Calmly I live, no earthly ties have I ;
My art alone, and my philosophy
Dwell in my soul ; she dreams as yet, but soon
Will break the golden fetters of her sleep,
And try her pinions 'mid humanity.'—
He paused, and she, her sweet voice quivering,
Told him her story ; how in Italy
The fragile blossom of her mother's life
Had faded into death ; her father's heart
Drew him with force resistless after her,
And she, their love-crown, was brought home across
The wailing sea to her dead mother's land,

An orphan and a stranger :—wealth she had,
And friends as the world counts them ; but they
    sought
To form her, as they called it, for the life
Of fashion, and unheard, to drown in her
All those pure yearnings for sublimity,
And action in the struggle, which she felt
Ripple the calmness of her virgin mind ;
A strife to reach the higher peaks of life,
Not simply vegetate in the low vale.—
He listened; and then questioned eagerly,
With heart aflame, on which the falling tones
Of her low voice dropped incense-like to depths
Unfelt before, and raised a glory mist
Of rapturous new feelings ;—so they stood
Forgetful of all else ; the moonlight fair
Gleamed on their upturned faces silently ;
They talked ; not merely babbled, letting swim
A bubble weather-wisdom down the tide
(In subtle evolution) of their speech,
And hiding 'neath the courtesy of tone,
And slow correctness of a lazy drawl,
Their emptiness of feeling, and of aim :—
Far different their words ; from heart to heart
The wing of speech flew swift, and answer found
Ere resting-place was reached : two souls had met
This moonlight eve, 'mid dreams of holy grail,
And angels sweeping thro' the gleaming blue,
Whose clasping fingers typified the bond
Of love which clasped their hearts—for evermore.—
She was no fragile blossom, floating down
The lilied stream of life ; a beauteous gem

Fit only for man's royal diadem,
To dazzle and no more ; beauty she had,
A glorious richness of full loveliness
To light up death with, and to gladden life—
The wayside life of mortals, not of kings.
She was a flower whose rich colour-crown
Flashed on the portals of each passing heart
And filled them with rare music, echoing
The chorus of the stars ; but far beyond
The beauty of her face, and melody
Of her most rhythmic form, lay richer gifts
But shadowed forth in these—a soul so pure,
And so intensely loving, that it twined
Round merest life-wreck, with ideal grace
Transfiguring the bareness :—and for him,
We know the poetry of thought and deed
Which clasped hands in his heart ; and so the two
Flashed into friendship, with a gleam of stars,
A radiance of moonlight, and a breeze
Of music whisp'ring from the swinging pines.—
Each day which chased its brother down the gold
Of the world's life thread held a pearl for them
To count the time by : so the summer passed ;
And his heart numbered in its precious shrine
The hours marked by her presence : 'such a one
She musing stood, while I played Lohengrin ;'
'Ah ! then we wandered hand in hand among
The waving fern blades underneath the pines ;'
Or, 'the day passed without her, but at eve,
As wailing music stole from my sad soul,
Her presence blessed me with its blissfulness ;'
And so with everyone until the end.—

But summer blooms not always, and at last
The gorgeous wreaths of autumn passed away
With fruition's swift pace, and left the ground
Weeping and sad for beauty desolate ;
And winter dawned with sad prefigurement
Of parting and of sorrow—still she came ;
And still their souls grew closer for the fear
Which lurked in each, a changing doubt in his—
A certainty in hers—that they must part,
Or that sublime endeavour for mankind
Would ne'er outblossom from their happy hearts.—
One evening when they met, he said no word
Of usual greeting, but his fingers strayed
Among the tangled sweetness of the notes
And drew forth a love-song—a curtain hung
Before them on the wall ; the silken hue
Of cloudless heav'n bore ' Hope' in silver thread
Upon its azure—but he spoke not yet
And sang on with a passionate deep voice :—

    ' My heart has blossomed ; behold the love flow'r,
      I offer it unto thee ;
    May its fragrance sweeten the passing hour
      And dwell in thy memory !

    ' By it may my soul to thine own speak clear,
      Or sweet, oh crown of the strife !
    Wilt thou wear my blossom each passing year,
      And bless with thy love my life ?

    ' Oh lily-fair heart ! oh divine rapt eyes !
      Oh beauty beyond compare !

Oh rapture of loving that slumb'ring lies
   Caught in mesh of golden hair !


' Be mine, be mine own : and I dare to win
   A laurel wreath for thy brow ;
I will storm fame's height, I will enter in,
   And my name, unknown till now,


' Shall ring thro' the earth with a mighty sound,
   And all men triumphantly
Shall greet the fair treasure my life has found :
   Oh love, give thyself to me ! '


Then sinking into minor, that gay song
Fell dropping with a tender monotone
Of rippling treble, like a human sigh
Too deeply felt for speaking.   So it ran :—


   ' Oh love me, my belovèd,
      Love but me,
      But me alone !
      For I love thee
      With every tone
My life can quiver from its soul's deep chords.
      Oh love me, my belovèd,
      Love but me !


' Oh lily of the pine wood, on my brow
      Pour gently down,
      My sweetest now,
      Thy fair love-crown ;

And coolness of thy kisses ; that they drown
  All other sound
  Amid their blisses.
  With a bound
My soul springs up to greet thee ;
 Oh belovèd, love me,
  Love but me,
  But me alone !
 Oh love me, my belovèd,
  Love but me !'

In faintest murmurs died the song away,
And answerless it swept adown the air;
Then turned he and straight gazed into her eyes,
And drew the silken curtain from the wall,
The cloud which hid the blossom ;—there it hung,
His deep soul speaking out of his art's might ;
A revelation of love's pow'r in him,
A pleading strong—half-irresistible.—
'Twas cloudy moonlight, breaking into gleams
Of silver whiteness thro' black shadowing,
Within the picture ; and a mountain stood
Clear in the light, snow-topped with rugged sides,
And jagged cliffs, whose darkness seemed a fear,
A shudder, and a warning ; no path led,
At the first gazing, up the precipice,
While far below a swirling torrent rushed
In utter wild abandonment, and bore
Amid its foam torn blossoms down the stream ;
And hurled high trees from forests in its flow
Mad surging on resistless ;—but the eye
Grown soon familiar with the gloominess,

And darkness of the scene, began to trace
The merest shadow of steps, ruggedly
Up-creeping thro' the snow ; so faint they were,
So slipp'ry gleaming in the changing light,
It seemed impossible a human foot
Could mount their dizziness, yet on the track
A pilgrim stood, with frail staff firmly grasped
In guiding hand, and deep and tender eyes
Raising their mute pathetic hopefulness
To cloud-capped summit with its crown of stars :
And as the gaze (grown clearer) followed his
In its dumb rapture of expectancy,
The clouds rolled into order, and disclosed
(As 'neath a veil) a lonely woman's form,
Tall, beautiful, and calm, with hair back flung
Upon the pinions of the waiting breeze,
And eyes down-drooping to the wanderer ;
A crown of laurel in her outstretched hand
She held towards him, with the tender smile
Of waiting rapture knowing well the end.—
' Oh love,' he said, ' a cloud is o'er thy face ;
I cannot see those eyes bent down on me
For drooping lids ; oh lift the veil away
And shine forth, in my heart full-blossoming ! '
He turned, and lo ! a mistiness of tears
Drowned the blue sweetness of the deepest eyes
Which ever mirrowed heav'n to lover's sight :
A passion swept his spirit, like a breath
Of the night breezes rushing thro' the pines,
And standing straight with rapturous unrest
He seized her quiv'ring to his throbbing heart,
And with the might of kisses calmed away

The glist'ning rain-veil of her loveliness,
And pressed his warm lips on her rose-like mouth
As if to stifle aught but answ'ring kiss :—
Yet pale she grew, as for a moment clung
Her lips to his in love's forgetfulness :
Then gently slipping from his arms' fond clasp
She stood a marble type of innocence,
And answered with a sob which caught her voice
And crushed its sweetness to monotony :
' Not so, oh love ; it is not happiness
Which gains life's highest crown ; it is not love,
But suffering alone which raises us
Unto the brightness of the mountain peak,
And fair glow of the stars—ah not in vain
The lessons of thy grand philosophy,
And most sublime art-teaching ! Do we not
Both hold the faith, of possibility
For highest climbing in the lowest worm,
Tho' waiting springtide of development
In slumbering heart? Oh love, and can we not
Make our strong faith stand forth in stronger deeds.
And lead the march of triumph on its way?
I dare not think, oh love—I dare not pause—
Too weak my heart, too wholly thine ! I know
The right stands clear before me, dare I choose
The pleasant and the happy, here with thee ?
What peace can dwell with shadow of a grave
O'ercasting it for ever ?—Oh my love,
Would not our noblest feelings lie entombed ?
Our highest, purest aims be buried deep
Beneath the grave of earthly happiness ?
The acted lie is ever more accursed

Than the outspoken one, for that can be
With truth confronted till it fall to dust,
And all lies die, swift pierced by heaven's light ;
But oh, belovèd, would the acted lie
Of stifling in our souls the solemn truth
The stedfast stars, the everlasting hills,
The blueness silver-flecked of moonlight eve,
And rapture of the sun-dawn gave to us—
Would that die soon unnoticed, echoless?
No ; rather would it drag the coming souls,
Who felt like us the possibility
Of higher climbing, down to common earth,
If we, apostles of the dawning truth,
Cast down our inspiration, and our crown
For a mere wreath of fading earthly blooms.
Oh love, my soul is stedfast, but my heart
Holds thee alone, and will not let thee go !
My love ! my love ! so brave, so fetterless—
So gentle yet so strong—oh pity me !
I cannot reach thy stature, but I feel
Its might and majesty of godliness—
I know the glorious fate which hangs for thee
Unknown in some fair star ; go forth, oh love,
Go forth and struggle for the nobleness
Thou feelest in thy soul, and know'st thereby
Humanity bears veiled and slumbering
Until the word is spoken, and it burst
In mighty purple bloom ; the thistle crown—
The passionate rich heart behind the pricks.
I dare not drag thee down, oh love ! oh love !
And yet I never knew what bitterness
Lay hidden in this hour !—Farewell my love !

I cannot say more now—my heart will break ;
But when full seven days have chased away
This weakness, I will come, and meet thee here,
And then no more, oh never any more,
Thro' all the long days of eternity ! '
A sob drowned her sweet voice, and turning swift
She fled adown the pine trees' shadowing
Like hope before despair, and he, alone,
Let fall the curtain o'er his bloom of art
And dimly groped in his soul's bitterness
For star to pierce the darkness, and none came.
Without her what was life ? an empty void—
Philosophy a dream—and art a curse,
Since with its beauty it still back recalled
The vanished hopeless beauty of his love.—
Deep night fell o'er his spirit, and he felt
The direful tempting every soul must know
Who lives beyond the usual, and can taste
The rapture and the thirst undying, fierce,
For the eternity which dwells beyond
Our seeking, yet puts forth a thrill of pain
In every passion which can rise above
The commonplace, and lose sight of itself
In reckless torment of that shadow grasp.
Death stood beside him, still and beautiful,
A mystic weaving shade of loveliness—
A flicker of white moonlight hid the eyes
So cold and pitiless, and made them gleam
Like dewy blossoms on a rippling stream ;
She laid her cool white hand on his hot brow,
And whispered with the rhythmic hopelessness
Of her low voice, to weary souls so sweet :

' Linger not—tarry not—
  Come to me swift ;
Life holds no joy for thee
  Sweet as my gift ;
Peace—sorrow, out of sight—
Rest—after life's hard fight.

' Whisper low, ere I go,
  Thy heart shall steep
In all the blissfulness
  Of slumber deep :
Tirèd soul, come to me ;
Toss not on life's rough sea.

' All thy high dreams must die,
  Why not then thou ?
Life wears no happiness
  To crown thy brow
Like that sweet rest of mine—
Mortal, become divine !

' Doth not every whisper of the pine-boughs—
    Doth not every sighing of the leaves—
Every murmur as the wailing wind soughs
    Thro' the fragile blossoms which it grieves—
Every ray of moonlight falling faintly—
    Every bird with weary song to morn—
Every human brow, tho' high and saintly,
    Curse the wretched hour when it was born?

' Mortal, let thy spirit sink to slumber,
    Let my cooling hand upon thy brow

Give thee calm and blisses without number ;
    Lean thy aching heart upon me now.
Life is but a weariness ; and living
    Beareth ever a sharp stinging pain ;
Peace can never blossom but in giving
    Soul and form to nothingness again ! '


So Death low-murmured, letting fall a sound
Cool as the night wind on his aching brow ;
Then silently she waited that her words
Might bud, and grow to their own fruition. —
Oh Death, so witching fair to the sad soul
With wooing sweet white arms and peace-crowned
    brow,
Thou would'st have conquered in that hour of woe,
Of hopes downcast, and fair dreams ruthlessly
Torn up by their strong roots and cast adown
The precipice of fate—but heedlessly
And half despairing in the conflict, he
Struck forth his hands, and striking touched the keys
Whose music ever vanquished his heart plague—
A note flashed forth, a tone of Lohengrin,
Where snowy angels float down the far blue
In mystic bearing of the holy grail ;
A mist fell from his spirit, and he knew
The horror of the Death so near his heart
With icy fingers clutching at his brow,
And shook her from him, and rose strengthenèd;
Then passed into the night and wandered on
Beneath the moaning pine-boughs where the stars
Were blotted out by umbrage of thick leaves :
No sound struck on the stillness save the sigh

Of these same breeze-blown branches, whispering
A faintest requiem for his loneliness :—
He sought in Nature gracious comforting,
Nor sought in vain ; the poet ever finds
A healing blessing in her silences—
A throbbing rapture in her breathlessness,
Which raises him beyond the present ill
To distant future brightness.   Ah that gift,
That blessèd gift, of art ! that nature throb—
That solace of all sorrow, that pure joy ;
That revelation of all mysteries
In human darkened life—to those who bear
This blessing in their souls the deepest woes
Fall powerless to crucify; they feel,
Even in sharpest anguish, a faint glimpse
Of ever-brightening glory, which can still
The thrilling of humanity to rest !—
The seven dragging days passed by at last,
And left their crust of healing on his mind ;
Time's gentle fingers never pass in vain
Their soft caressing touch on weary brows,
But leave them cooler for their sympathy,
Unheard, but felt thro' every quivering nerve :
Ah would that human sympathy were deep
And voiceless as the years' ! true sympathy
Can never speak its sorrow, but in deeds
Lets fall the dew of healing on the bloom
Of life down-crushed by anguish—when our souls
Half maddened by the conflict tired sink
To rest awhile in sadness, and lay down
The growing burden which our spirits bear,
A look may comfort, a caressing touch,

But words — ah words are poisoned burning
   draughts,
And fire sparks dropped into the open wound,
A torture, and a tempting to cast down
Life's self upon its burden ! Careless words
Falling across our life at every step,
How wondrous is their power ! like butterflies
They glad youth's summer day and float above
The perfumed flow'rs in beauty and in love,
Making the earth a very paradise
While our hearts echo ; but alas how soon
Like poisoned wasps they sting our spirits bare !
The butterflies have fled, the buzzing swarm
Of word tormentors wear the night away.—
Again 'twas eventide, the seventh eve
(From that one branded on my artist's soul
With scorching letters) gloomed at last in tears,
As if to sympathise with her sad heart :
She came between the dark boughs silently;
A mistiness of raindrops, and a wave
Of rushing sadness from the surging pines,
These were her welcome ; to the happy heart
A low pathetic poem ; but her soul,
Torn with the struggle, anguished with regret,
Felt but the moaning of its hopelessness ;
The tragedy of living pierced her thro' ;
The bearing of life's burden pressed her down
To merest helplessness of wondering
When would the end come ? but the woman soul
Is ever instinct with the bearing grief,
Not casting it impatient down the far
Of death-illusion—is it weakness this ?

I know not ; but the man's thought ever is
To toss life down ; the woman's, to endure—
Perhaps 'tis cowardice, a fear to strike ;
Perchance 'tis nobleness, a feeling strong,
Deep-rooted in some minds, that holiness
Is born in suffering, and rendered pure
By patiently worn sorrow ; and now ' Dream '
(So had my artist named her) came adown
The dripping forest with a will resolved
To bear his sorrow (harder than her own),
Yet to be stedfast for the sacrifice.—
He saw her coming, and sprang forth to greet
With clasping hand the coldness of her own,
Which met his for the parting : so they stood,
Their faces passion pale ! no moonlight gleam
Of glory on the fairness of their brows ;
No calmness of the stars in their wild eyes :
And neither spoke : too great the agony
For mortal words to speak it ; hand clasped hand
As if the holding of the fingers twined
Could distance parting, and ward off despair :—
Sky's falling tears mixed with the human ones
Which drifted down her cheeks ; the moaning winds
Rushed wailing thro' the wood ; no other sound
Disturbed the silence ; but the surging clouds
Tossed rudderless and aimless thro' the air :
Both at the same quick time-flash wandered back
To that first eve of meeting, and their hands
Unknowing grasped more close ; a whisper might
Of bygone rapture flooded all his soul,
And loosed his tongue, and he burst suddenly
Into a chainless tide of burning speech :

' Oh my belovèd, speak !   Dost thou not know
    I cannot let thee go ?
I cannot, 'tis impossible !   Oh see,
    What now remains for me
If thou, my love, dost leave me ! all in vain,
    And breathing but of pain,
My art, my life, my grand philosophy—
    I give them up for thee !
Oh whisper not of parting, my heart's star !
    Gleam down the distant far
Of my life's blackness, making it to glow
    With love our sad hearts know.
Shine not alone, my darling, stay with me !
    What am I without thee ?
A cloud wind-driven—a strong tree uptorn ;
    Ah better never born,
Than cast adrift when most I feel the pain
    Of life so cold and vain :
My soul's one love, I will not let thee go ;
    Thou shalt not leave me so !
Ah my art's dream of beauty, tinging all
    On which thy look did fall
With that sweet soul outshining thro' those eyes !
    Gaze not in sad surprise
At my wild passion springing into speech ;
    I fall down, and beseech,
In merest whisper, that thou leave not me,
    I have no world but thee ;
No life, no hope, no aim ; mere helplessness
    (Unless thy lips will press
My cold ones into being) weighs me down ;
    Life holds for me no crown

Unless thy love can reach it from the height
    Beyond my blinded sight,
Unless thy beauty be my ladder fine,
    And lighted lamp to shine
Thro' blackness of the air, and give it me.
    Oh love, I kneel to thee ;
Oh leave me not in darkness ; nay, I swear
    Thou shalt not leave me there !
Thou shalt be mine, I swear it; and thy heart
    Bears in its inmost part
A blessing on my daring ; for I know
    The love within says, " No ; "
'Tis but the will to bear and sacrifice,
    (No matter at what price)
Thy happiness for duty, which impels
    What thy sweet face out-tells
Is anguish to thy spirit : oh my love,
    Raise thy fair height above
This madness of denial ; as we two stand
    Hand locked in clasping hand,
So let us pass thro' life, and let our dreams
    Like two uniting streams
Whose waters joined, flow on with stronger sound,
    And more resistless bound,
And brave the heat of scorching summer-glow
    To stop their gentle flow,
Because they rush together to the sea ;
    Thus through eternity
Let our lives flow together ; oh my sweet,
    My feeble words repeat,
And still repeat, this burden, " leave not me ; "
    I perish without thee !

I struggle for expression to make clear
    The beauty of the near,
Of love, of happiness ; oh sweet ! the " far,"
    Be it a distant star,
Or merely earthly wreck, cannot compare
    With joy of present fair ;
I strive to speak it, but how small a part
    Up-surging in each heart
Can find expression in mere earthly speech :
    My wailing looks beseech
What dwells beyond my asking ;—I have done :
    Love, have I lost, or won ? '
She raised her sad eyes to his glowing face
With mute denial, half drowned in tenderness :
' It is because I love thee, I say " lost " '
(Fell from her pale lips down the sighing wind) ;
' It is because I would not have thee lose,
For sweetness of the present, future bliss,
Which comes in climbing up the heights of life
And proving humanness can raise itself
To the fair stars : it is for this, oh love,
That my voice murmurs brokenly, but firm,
" Lost ! lost for ever :" thy philosophy
Has entered in my soul, and dwelleth there,
Transmuting littleness and ignorance
To high endeavour and clear-sightedness.—
Scorn not the earth ; despise not daily joys ;
No ladder that, to reach the distant sky ;
Heav'n will be realised, and truly known,
When earth is understood—not trodden down,
But raised, and purified, and blossoming !—
When human souls have learned the nobleness

Which makes a crime impossible, disease
And misery unknown; 'tis our false thoughts,
Our base desires, our meanness and our sin,
Which hinder human blooming into god,
And earth becoming heaven : the hour dawns
When human souls will shudder, looking back
To this same present we so haughtily
Hold crowned and conquering, and call the time
A hideous dream of darkness; when the child
Shall no more drink with unpolluted breath
The fœtid air of soul-destroying creeds,
And baseless superstitions making life
A mere graveyard for stumbling; then indeed,
When sovereign mind shall choose its own pure food
Adulterate no more, but nourishing
To highest peaks of knowledge undismayed
By spectres of dead giants, life will be
A gift worth holding, a fair thistle-bloom
To crown our human brows !   How few there are
Who feel this boundless possibility
In commonplace of life : but we, oh love,
We know it, and must bear it different ways,
Unheeding that our life paths separate
And join not until death.   Oh love ! oh love !
Farewell, farewell ! yea farewell evermore !
My passing spirit will unite with thine
And draw thee to me when death reaches us.'—
Her low tones dropped to silence, and far off
Seen dimly thro' the rain-flecked looming sky
A faintest glimmer of the wannest gold
Stole, half afraid to greet the coming morn,
And pierced the weeping clouds, and down the east

Rose like the promise of eternity
Beyond the mist of death—a great calm fell
Across the wailing branches, and they paused
To marvel where the torturing wind had flown
Which lashed them into madness through the night ,
And a mere shadow of half-veilèd sound
Came from the drowsy birds still slumbering
Yet singing 'mid their dreams.   All agony
Must sink at last to silence, and a time
Comes in all sorrow when the sharpest pang
Fails to disturb the calmness.   Hopelessly,
But dumbly, did he loose her claspèd hand
And let it flutter from his clinging grasp
To wander o'er the earth, or find its rest
Beneath the canopy of heaven's stars.—
And so they parted, with no farewell kiss
Of passionate mute love to gleam adown
The darkness of their path, a flash of light
In which the bare bleak years stood glimmering :
And she alone passed from beneath the pines
Which silent stood, and musical no more
Sang neither song of woe or joyfulness :
Her light feet trod the heather brown and sere
And glided o'er the grass blades up the hill
Into the silence of her dwelling place ;
He watched her slipping from his yearning sight,
And saw the dull days rise and wane, and still
His life stretched boundless, on a level plain,
No glints of sunlight on its hopelessness ;
His spirit bowed beneath the agony,
And turning, as the tired soul ever will
Unto the deepest passion which it knows,

His fingers sought the keys which sang to him
In happy days of grand ideal art,
Of love, philosophy, and all that we
Bear highest in our minds.   Is there aught here
Which music cannot soothe? her wordless tone
Of sympathy falls sweeter on our ears,
And opens our heart portals silently
With precious healing overflowing all
The wreck-strewn shore of life—than any word
The dearest and the truest of our kind
Can ever speak, with wet eyes and soft hand
Seeking to soothe what is unsoothable
Except by time, and music ; for the mind,
Borne high above the common tide of life
By wave of anguish, raises up unknown
Its stature to the universal height
Of the great world-soul, ' possibility,'
And only in the union with pure truth
Can find surcease for sorrow of the ' now.'—
When the wan dawn had brightened into day
He left his stedfast pine-wood, and sped on
Across the bare brown heather, and the grass,
Whose dewdrops fastened on his eager feet
As if to drag them backward, but in vain :
He passed the hill, his beacon point till now,
With stern denial of gazing, for she dwelt
Upon its summit, and he dare not see
Her eyes again, or they would chain him there.
And so he left behind him his fair youth,
And art-dreams for reality ; and strode
Down to the world from great heights of his love.
And there we leave him, but shall catch again

The gold thread of his life, unravelling
His sorrows, and his aim to light mankind
To the fair distance of true holiness
And mountain peak of stars, and gleaming blue
Of over-arching sky above their brows.
And her strife in the petty narrowness
The usual woman life must circle thro',
And count it blessing that the storms of fate
Or glory rapture crowning manly brows
Are shielded from her weakness ; count it bliss
If one of these same crowned ones offer her
The blessèd title to make glad his life,
And rule his house, and decorate his feasts,
And bear his humours patiently, and serve
Her lord and master, until the death hour
Shall sound releasing from the torturer !
Their life threads yet may cross in distant time,
Each seeking to express the soul's deep thoughts
In deeper deeds of loving sufferance ;
And striving with the leaven of their minds
To fuse the whole dull lump of humanness
To living genius—borne above the clay
Of their base natures trailing thro' earth-dust.

---

## PART II.

THE years toiled on with agèd, halting feet,
Up the steep gorge of dusk eternity,
And left their footsteps carvèd in the stone,
Some firm and lasting, others dim and pale,
And half effaced by following rough years
Who trod them down with scoffing out of sight :
And these years caught my artist and left him,
As one by one they passed, more desolate ;
With less of hope, but more of firm resolve
Graved on his brow, and lighting up his eyes.
He roamed across the world, and ever strove
To make men listen to the singing stars,
And live, not vegetate, and call it life !
He learned their hand-crafts, and their brain-crafts
    too,
And sought the usual and the commonplace,
The hills and vales of life ; but ever found
Himself mocked as a dreamer, and his creed
The scoffing butt of fools : he sang to them ;
He borrowed music's pleading, stronger far
Than any human word ; they listened calm
And praised the artist, but ignored the man ;
Or shrugging scornful shoulders muttered low :
' A genius' skull is ever full of dust
To fly in reason's eyes, and blind the sight
For daily human life ; mark not his words,
But hear his gift of music readily.'
And so the blind world heard him willingly,

When music pleaded at their deafened hearts,
But understood not what the music meant,
Or why its might so pierced them that they came
Again, and yet again to hear the voice
Which, singing, swayed their souls, but speaking truth,
The music's utterance, in human speech,
Fell echoless adown their barren lives.—
One man there was in all the multitude
Who listened when he spoke with longing eyes
Half grasping with their yearning at his words
The sweetness of the truth beyond the rind :
And one day as he stood with distant gaze,
Oblivious of all save the far blue
Of skyward dreaming where his spirit roamed,
My artist drew towards him, and with tone
Of softest sympathy held out his hand ;
A yearning for the fellowship of man
Came with resistless surging o'er his soul
So high and desolate among mankind ;
He felt this heart bore kindred with his own,
A germ of brighter possibility
Lay hid in those deep eyes : ' Oh friend,' he said,
' I know that nobleness abides in you,
I feel its echo striking from your soul,
Straight to the depths of mine ; oh dream no more,
Speak to me clear ; I know the aim is high
Beneath that thoughtful brow : have you found truth?
Oh hold her light across me, that her rays
Fall on the darkness, ever unexplored
Of humanness beneath my spoken word ;
If I can teach you, see how willingly

My thoughts are yours, my hopes, my aims, my voice—
Speak then, oh brother ! take my hand in thine,
The grasp of fellowship gives mighty pow'r
'To every human soul to bear and do !'
The deep eyes turned the pathos of their look
Straight on my artist, and with monotone
Of wearied sadness, answered his appeal :

' At dawn of life, I might have raised
    A name the wise had loved to bless,
My truth-filled poems had been praised,
    My wisdom lauded to excess ;

' I felt the fiery touch had given
    Unto my brow a crown of rays,
Which, if to burnish I had striven,
    Had lit up all the after days :

' My thoughts sprang forth half wing'd to heav'n ;
    Had I sustained their early flight,
They soon had lost the dull earth's leav'n,
    And soared above in perfect light.

' Alas ! alas ! I might have sung
    The martyr's hope, the hero's fame ;
My sounding verses might have rung           .
    For ever with fair freedom's name :

' All this (nay more) I might have done,
    My soul had pow'r to strive and gain,
But never was aught precious won
    By counting cost, or heeding pain ;

‘ For while I waited, watching flow
   The strong waves of life's swift river,
My hour had time to come, and go
   Again to the mighty giver ;

‘ And still tho’ indolent and slow,
   I might have caught its burning pow'r,
But that another magic glow
   Swept o’er my spirit at that hour :

‘ Love flew in with wings outspread ;
         Love the fair,
         The sweetly smiling ;
         With radiant hair,
   And soft low voice my sense beguiling :

‘ Alas ! how often had I heard and read
Of just such coming, yet it seemed to me
· A grand new dream, wonder and mystery !
And ever as a wave draws to the shore,
And melts away all landmarks ; more and more
My soul drank that sweet poison, and lost count
Of all the many steps it had to mount
Before the god-like heights of fame were reached.

   ‘ Love with a halo round her head,
            A purple mist
            Like amethyst,
   Flew, steeped in perfume o’er my waning sense ;
            How could I wait?
            I felt my fate
   And kneeling low resigned all vain defence :

Then light beamed round
O'er all the ground,
And filled the earth with beauty, me with bliss :
My soul woke blind,
How could I find
The heights of glory bartered for a kiss?
The kiss was sweet :
It is but meet,
Since love has blessed me, I should give her praise ;
The vow she took
With her fair look
Has ne'er been broken thro' the passing days :
Yet still I long
For that wild song
My soul could hear in youth's days long ago ;
It is not best
Just to find rest,
And inspiration cometh but from woe !
'Tis when the soul
Beyond control
Has lost itself in sea of agony,
That, maimed and worn,
Its flight is borne
By angels, thro' time to eternity ;
So journeying
On spirit's wing
Can hear, and drink, the music of the spheres ;
And then can sing
To us within
The prison-house below—the vale of tears :
And ring thro' time
With mystic rime,
Leading men on to glory, or the grave,

And sounding clear,
That all may hear
Who dare the witching looks of love to brave ;
And cast away
Her magic sway
To choose a nobler lot :—no light or glow,
No thrilling kiss
Of love, nor bliss
Of rapture, which she lends to all below,
Can e'er compare
(For those who dare
To gaze but on the stars, nor heed her song)
With that soul-voice !
Oh had my choice
But kept to that, for which I ever long !
Love's rosy crown
I would cast down,
And be alone, my visions only near,
Could I but now
Feel on my brow
The crown of inspiration ; could I hear
That mystic rime
In youth's fair time
So near me : falling on my spirit free
As summer rain ;
But ne'er again
Will God be near me as he used to be.
Repentance late,
And moans at fate,
May make life bitter, but can ne'er repair
The ruin wrought
By want of thought
And passion's voices followed without care.

Yet it may be
I still shall see
In some more blessèd life that hour again,
And then shall know
Before it go
Soul pleasures only bring no yearning pain!'
'Oh brother,' said my artist, 'is not love
The highest inspiration?   I had lost
All other hope, how willingly for her!
Tho' swift denial met all my pleading heart
And crushed it into silence, yet my creed
Was ever, that love purifies the soul
And raises it beyond the present gift
Of dear possession to th' eternal stars.'
'Nay, rather does it chain to this dull earth
The soaring soul if ever realised;'
Made answer wearily the saddened voice :
'It is but while a dream, unknown, untouched—
And bearing still the magic rarity
Of growing beyond reach—that it can raise
To its own height of blooming ; and that height
Is not reality, but semblance fair
We ever feign to gift our ideal ;
Once let us reach it, wear it as our own,
Alas, from a bright star which led us on
Across the swamps of life to the far hill
Of nobleness and glory, it will shrink
Into a sharp and stinging fetter point
Struck thro' our souls to pin them to the earth.
Speak no more to me ; offer me no more
The hand of fellowship ; my home is here ;
But yours is far beyond ; eternity

Lies waiting for your presence; never more
Will I hear your tone's magic, which recalls
The beauty of the past—in hopelessness ! '—
And turning with no parting farewell word
He passed into the darkness; and unknown,
Unseen again, sped down the distant night
Of human life's forgetfulness; and he
Who would have sought a brother, heard instead
An echo of his Dream's words bitterly
Float over from the past :—so he toiled on
To other lands, and other humanness,
And myriad development of life
With the same spirit hid beneath the veil ;
The same hard scoff at holiness and truth,
The same contemptuous sentence ; ' he is mad'!
On all his fervent words, and deeds, and thoughts—
Yet he still struggled with a deathless love—
A stern repression of earth's weaknesses ;
And strove (nor vainly) on his human brows
To wear the calmness of the stedfast stars,
And hold the deepness of infinity
Within his patient eyes ;—and she his Dream
Reigned always in his heart, and reigned alone ;
A sweet pathetic memory of bliss
Felt clearly in all beauty ; greeting him
At midnight 'neath the glory of the moon,
And rapture of the stars, and floating clouds,
By soft breeze whisper, and hushed brooklet's sound,
And perfumed pray'r of blossom, and each tone
Revealing Nature to her worshipper :—
His thoughts sprang into music sad and low,
Its sweetness melting into silences

With feeling rhythm quivering all thro' :
(Our words flash forth in poems, constantly
When a great passion sways us ; be it joy,
Or anguish, 'tis the same ; the breath divine
Which raises us beyond the commonplace,
And makes us one with Nature, gifts our voice
With music like her own, to shadow forth
The human and the god in unison !)

     ' Tho' thy presence is to me
     But a sad sweet memory,
     Yet more high and holily
         Fair my love, I love thee.

     ' When the night breeze sweeps adown
     From the hill-top's snowy crown,
     And across the heather brown,
         Fair my love, I love thee.

     ' When the calmness of the stars
     Shines thro' my life's prison bars,
     Gleaming from the dim " afars "
         Fair my love, I love thee.

     ' When my soul, half in despair,
     Doubts if glory heights compare
     With the vales so cool and fair ;
         Sweet my love, I love thee.

     ' When on wings of music borne,
     My weak spirit sad and worn
     Dreams it is not left forlorn :
         Sweet my love, I love thee.

'When I see the blossoms round
Spread their beauty o'er hard ground,
Seeking soul, and having found :
      Sweet my love, I love thee.

' Oh my love, the mystery
Which the green leaves sing to me
Is but shadowing of thee !
      Pure my love, I love thee.

' 'Mid the mystic silentness
Of the earth's vast wilderness,
Where no mouth my lips dare press,
      Pure my love, I love thee.

' Never love-clasp glads my own,
And no other's look or tone
Have I sought, save thine alone !
      Pure my love, I love thee.

' Tho' I know my eye in thine
Ne'er may see the answ'ring shine
Of true love which is divine,
      Yet, my love, I love thee.

' When pale death with noiseless feet
Shall our hearts with coldness greet,
Then, and then alone, oh sweet,
      I dare prove I love thee !

' Then my life, its struggle past,
Peaceful lies, but holds thee fast ;
Oh my love ! my own at last,
      I dare prove I love thee !

' Then that kiss we never knew
Pierces the last anguish thro' ;
Death is rapture borne with you !
I dare prove I love thee.'

So he sang on, but sudden sprang upright,
For borne upon the night breeze faint and low
A kiss flashed on his lips : and murmur wan
Came floating down the stillness of the wood,
The merest whisper, of a woman's sigh
Heard far off in the blueness of the hills :
He knew it for the summons she had pledged :
' Farewell ! farewell ! yea, farewell evermore !
My passing spirit will unite with thine,
And draw thee to me, when death reaches us : '
So had she spoken ; and the time had come,
The blossom of the thistle to his soul ;
And he sped onward, counting each time-flash
A jewel lost, which parted him from her.—
At last he reached the pinewood, and again
Passed swift beneath its branches, the same man
To outward seeming who had dwelt there once ;
But oh how different !   Then, art was life,
And dreams a glory, and the life, a crown ;
Pure happiness a possibility—
Earth, heaven's germ, and humanness, a star
Of nobleness and fame ; while now, alas !
Naught of these jewels bound his weary brows
Save life alone, a woven wreath of thorns !
The swinging pine boughs murmured constantly
Their old refrain, but hopelessly and sad,
And answerless for ever, to his soul.

But he passed on unheeding, and came out
Upon the moorland, where the heather bloom
Had faded into blackness ; and the grass
Hung, waving tattered banners of defeat :
He crushed them without thinking, and sped on
Up the far hill, on which his Dream had dwelt,
And waited for his step with craving eyes
Whose death-like calmness melted into mist
Of sobbing tear-clouds when they met his gaze.
Serene she lay, and patient ; a soft couch
Of purple, wheeled into the window-space
Which opened to the ground, and let the gleam
Of tender moonlight flood the flowers pale
Of ling'ring monthly roses round its frame—
Was all the space her eager rhythmic form
Now circled on—so passionate before
In its lithe rapture of swift quivering
Adown the hills, and thro' the forest wide,
And o'er the springing heather's rosy bloom.—
They met, as they had parted, hand to hand
Close-clasping with a passionate hard grasp ;
And anguished eyes of his in calm of hers
De p-gazing silently—with not a word
Of greeting on their lips ; then he dropped down
Beside her on the ground, and whispered low,
' Is it so near, oh love ? so very near?
Wilt thou indeed be but a memory
Thro' all the coming years?   Art thou still free ?
Oh love, oh darling, let me kiss thy lips,
Then thou indeed art mine ! '   With warning hand
She prayed for silence, and then with a voice
Of tender sighing answerèd his pray'r :

' I am all thine, my love ; yea, thine and death's,
If thou care for my kisses ; but before
My mouth feels sweetness of thy answ'ring mouth
It must unveil its secrets.—Since that hour
When we two parted in the years gone by,
I never felt love-flash ; I heard indeed
Fair words of love, but ever answered them,
" Give me the hand of fellowship, oh man,
And not the kiss of love ! "    And strove to live
Up to the highest possibility
Thy art had taught me ; with philosophy
To crown my struggles, and make clear to all
The deep right lying hidden in our strifes,
Behind the present passion and the need :
I strove indeed to raise the woman-mind
Up to the heights, where men so calmly claim
The privilege of reigning ; while to us
They leave the low spots with o'ershadowing
From their most royal brows ; I strove indeed
For equal rights ; and freedom to evolve
His higher nature, for the labourer—
For light and air to all men's darkened souls—
But far beyond all this, and lying deep,
Almost too deep for grasping, did I strive
For that eternal abstract principle
Of justice in our souls, beyond the needs
Of present remedies for tyrannies :—
Till that be understood—till each one feels
The standard for true judgment does not lie
In what he thinks, in what his brother needs—
In what is best for nations, or for one—
But in what is above the present ill,

Above the daily thoughts, above our life—
Beyond all personal aims or ideas—
Almost above our holding ; but in truth
Not beyond reach of striving earnestness
To grasp and judge by, thro' eternity.
I thought to leaven with a spark of soul
One merely earthly nature, and to build
On this frail corner-stone my pyramid
Of glory for the race :—The man loved me
As best he could (or thought so) for the time ;
He was most plastic clay in my weak hands,
And I, poor fool, had visions of the crown
Of joy on human brows, which might outshine
The gleaming of the stars ; and gave myself
To bring life to the marble ; but alas,
The statue was but clay and rottenness !—
Ah poor hearts, poor hearts !   How I long to bless
    With a woman's kiss of love,
And a tender meaning of thoughts that press
    From the pitying sky above !
Poor souls toiling on, how I yearn to part
    Your sorrows between us here !
Oh brothers, your griefs I feel in my heart,
    Your wailing voices I hear !
Oh love, down-pressed by the thorns of life—
    Oh sore and wearying feet—
Can I never aid you amid the strife
And make word and action meet ?
This pleading ever-echoed in my soul,
Until I paused not to take count and see
If marble could be modelled from the clay
To strength and beauty by the godlike force

Of our philosophy, and art divine ;
But gave myself to purchase, as I thought,
His struggle with me for humanity !
Alas ! such ideals ever break beneath
The weight down-cast upon them—the time fled,
And his love fled before it down the days
Of our life-stream, grown flowerless and chill :—
He was a good man, as the world counts good—
He was a wise man, as the world holds wise—
And ever sought to love me, as he could,
And shield me from rough weather and life-storms ;
But when he found my spirit firmly set
Not with a child's heart but a woman's soul
On our grand life-aims, he would answer me
With a 'half-scornful wonder and a smile
Which stirred me into anger swift and hard
(Was I so weak that he should pity me ?)
And yet his words fell soft and music-like.
 One even when the moon did climb
  The arch of heav'n so calm and blue,
 My spirit tasting the sublime
  Did gaze the passing ages through ;
 And noted on the toilsome track
  Of life, the spirits pressing on ;
 While some gazed forward, some looked back,
  And some mused o'er their treasures won :
 But each whene'er he looked above,
  A shining statue, perfect, whole,
 And lovely, saw with looks of love
  Awaiting him at life's last goal :
 This statue was his perfect life
  As he might make it, and a sigh

Stole from his lips, " Ah me, the strife
  Will mar its beauty ere I die ! "
Yet still a thrill of rapture glowed,
  And lit up each pale bowed down face,
As they gazed on where downward flowed
  The sight of that exceeding grace.

·     ·     ·     ·     ·

But while I gazed at each wan form
  (Seen clearly by my spirit clear),
With all its sorrows 'mid life's storm
  Thus toiling on from year to year,
With all its hopes unguessed, unknown
  By the surrounding world ; its dreams
So scorned, and ever sentence thrown
  Not on what "*is*," but on what "*seems*" ;
A cloud passed o'er the scene, and I
  Had sudden reached the statue-land ;
It stood close to the far blue sky
  And stars gleamed thro' on either hand :
I looked ; and lo each toiler knelt
  Before the statue of his life,
Its image now, and yet there dwelt
  On each the tokens of the strife ;
The radiant beauty passing song
  Was marred and wrinkled, and the grace
Which to the statue did belong
  Had flown from the worn spirit's face ;
And one had lost the strong right hand ;
  And one was blind, and tears did fill
His sightless eyes ; and one did stand
  With pain comparing thought and will.

·     ·     ·     ·     ·

My heart was sad, for if there be
　　No grief so sharp as in despair
To see in thought the joys that we
　　Have known long since so sweet and fair ;
Yet still to feel the struggle o'er,
　　No chance again to fight or gain
A vict'ry, and that hope no more
　　May draw bright presages from pain ;
To know the time for struggle past,
　　And late repentance worse than vain ;
And feel the chains which fate has cast
　　Resistless as her iron reign :
This surely is enough to daunt
　　The boldest from the strife, and give
Some foothold for the scoffing taunt ;
　　" Is God a fiend who bids us live?
Who bids us struggle for a dream ?—
　　A shadow we can never reach—
While we bow to His will supreme,
　　And strive our aching souls to teach
That all we have, or hope, or gain,
　　Is but His love?—a God's to slaves !
Who godlike can rejoice in pain,
　　And with crushed hearts his sanctu'ry paves ?
My brothers, let us strive no more,
　　Heav'n has no bliss which can repay
The daily torment o'er and o'er
　　Returning with each dawning day,
But seize and taste the present bliss,
　　If bliss there be, and have no care
For future years ; love's offered kiss
　　Will make e'en anguish calm and fair !

We all must die, what matter how,
　　Or where? for dreaded, hoped, or wooed,
The moment comes ; the awful 'now'—
　　Which we must meet ; and, or subdued,
Or joyful, 'tis for all the same :
　　Some tears—a grave—perchance some love
More lasting may recall our name
　　To memory, when our tomb above
She passes ; but the praise, or blame,
　　Will little move the senseless dust !
A nation's tears—eternal fame—
　　What are they when grim death says ' must?'
Then strive not man to please, or God ;
　　Please but thyself, and take surcease
With pleasures gathered from the sod,
　　For strife which soon will end in peace ! "
My being rose in mutiny, and I
Hurled back his promises before the day
Of sacrifice (I called it) for a dream—
And he spoke calmly, almost wearily :
" You are a child, and know not what you need.
A woman's duty rarely lies beyond
Her own life circle, and her children's eyes ;
Those are her stars, and they should guide her way,
With no vain outward dreams.   Humanity
Can well support itself, and yields no grace
To those wild spirits who would spoil its peace ! "
Then turned and left me ; and I fell upon
The earth's cold bosom with most bitter tears !
My heart broke in that moment, for my dream
Alone had held me living without thee ;—
My love ! my love ! my godlike, noble love !—

I faded as the summer bore away
Her perfumed jewels, and my husband said
The distant Italy would call again
Spring roses to my cheeks, and so we went ;
Yet gathered no bright blooms in that fair land,
But only pale death-flowers !—He was brave,
And reckless like his nation; and one day
While a storm threatened, showed his fearlessness
And utter scorn of peril, and embarked
In a frail boat upon the surging sea,
Laughing and gay, and boasting he would bear
His vessel back to harbour in the calm :
He came indeed—the blue waves bore him back
Long ere the calm had settled over them,
With all his gaiety drowned out of him,
And death's calm on his brow:—I laid him down
Beneath the fragrant waving orange trees,
With requiem of blue sky and sighing air;
And then I sought the pinewood, and the hill,
Where we two met, and parted, years ago.
I waited patiently until I knew
My weary life grew very near its end,
And then my passing spirit summoned thine,
Oh true love, and thou heardest, and art here !—
Now kiss me ; lay thy fresh cool lips on mine
And let me so pass to eternity !'
Her tender voice sank mournfully to rest,
And he pressed all the passion of his soul
In that first love-kiss.   As rose-petals pale
Take a rich glow from sunlight wooing them,
So all the wanness of her quiv'ring mouth
Flashed into ruby brightness at his touch ;

She clung to him, the whole unlovely past
Since they two parted faded into dust ;
Again she felt young, happy, beautiful ;
And sprang up lightly with a passing strength :
' Oh love,' she said, ' let me hear Lohengrin
Once more, but this once more ; my spirit sees
The gleaming angels floating down the blue,
With perfumed presence of the holy grail ;
And yearns to join the song—oh sweetheart, play
That glorious dream again !'  Half-wild he stood
With anguish of the parting ; but he touched
With master-hand the keys, and shadowed forth
That wondrous revelation :—not a sound
Fluttered the stillness, till half unaware
The sweetness melted in the triumph-song
And rose sublime and strong—then a wild cry
Broke from her pallid lips : ' Oh love, my love,
Where art thou ? speak ; this blackness frightens me !
My hands grope blindly forth to find thy hands,
And miss them in the dark—where art thou, love?
Oh leave me not alone ! alone ! alone !'
Her voice pierced into shrillness at the end,
Then fell down into sudden silentness.
He sprang up madly, all his spirit's fear
Bursting in cry of anguish from his lips,
Now pale as hers, who lay so lifeless there.
He pressed her dead heart to his beating one ;
He held her cold mouth to his own warm lips,
And conjured her in wildest words of love
To open those sweet eyes, and look at him
Once more, but once !—Her dead heart gave no sign,
Her wan lips answered not his passionate

Wild raving of despair—in vain, in vain
The human seeks to dash itself against
The marble veil of death, and pierce beyond
(With the dear passing one) its mystery !—
His anguish sank to silence presently,
As passion ever must tho' true and real :
And he sought calmness in the wooing keys,
His only joy, his ruling love in death ;—
For death could not divide them ; when morn broke
They found the master cold, with fingers still
Upon the whiteness, breathing his swan-song.—
They bore the lovers to one resting place
Across the heather, to the stately pines
Whose swinging branches murmur constantly
Above their peaceful grave, and thistle-bloom
Springs from their loving hearts, a purple crown
Of deeper fuller blossom for their brows
Than any flower with mere sweetness fair,
Crushed into nothingness by careless hand,
And bearing 'neath its beauty no stern thorn
To beat the scoffer at its holiness
Back from its bosom, and develope thence
Beyond its bareness a triumphant crown !
And like the thistle our humanity
Bears hid within its soul the purple glow
Of fair development ; and each true heart
May hold the blossom of its nobleness
Before the eyes of men, until their minds
Spring by the gazing into fruition,
And heav'n is reached, for earth is understood !

## DULCAMARA.

'Twas long ago, as men count time,
  By days, and months, and years—
Yet not so long but that my rime
Can up the steep of mem'ry climb,
  And catch the dropping tears ;

And hold them with unanguished brow,
  Tho' sighing softly still ;
They bear no stinging sorrow now,
Tho' looking back I wonder how
  Such torture could not kill.—

Ah well ! time passes steadily
  And hardens as he goes ;
And tho' sometimes we readily
Could wish our bodies dead, that we
  Might sink in death's repose ;

Yet ere a year, or may-be two,
  Have slid into the past,
We catch a glimpse of heaven's blue,
Soft peeping all the darkness thro',
  E'en sorrow cannot last :

And Nature's blessèd voices fall,
 On tired hearts dropping down ;
The calm stars shine thro' heaven's wall,
And breathe their glow, and lighten all,
 And wan brows feel their crown ;

And every tiny bloom that springs—
. Or dew-drop on the grass ;
And every flutter of bird wings—
And every note that music sings—
 Wake echoes as they pass,

And bury with caressing tone
 Our sorrow out of sight ;
While every sigh, and every moan
Are whispering that not alone
 Nor outcast from the light,

We suffer, 'mid our pilgrimage
 In darkness drearily ;
There dwelleth One who can assuage
The tempest, tho' its wildness rage
 O'er our souls wearily ;

Else why instinctive do we cry,
 And lift our eyes above,
Nor turn below—but seek the high ?
Ah scoffers, tell the reason why,
 If not, that God is love !

And teaches us like creeping things,
 And twining fragile life,

To seek in climbing, budding wings
And grasp, and strike the angels' strings
    Clear harping thro' the strife.

They say, who deeply have down-gazed
    Thro' Nature's mysteries,
That every groping may be raised
To heights unknown, but not unpraised
    In poets' histories ;

And that the need bespeaks the power
    In plant, or tree, or man :
It may not be that one life-dower
Shall see the end, or fading flower
    Amid its blooming's span ;

But yet the race is strong to win,
    And triumphs at the last ;
For tho' in storms the springs begin
To let their freshness blossom in
    While skies are overcast ;

Yet soon the sunshine's golden hue
    Conquers the tempest's might,
And beam-like kisses down the blue
Slide sweetly to the rain-drop's dew
    And glorify their light !

And so from storm of unbelief,
    And tearing at the chain,
Whose end we miss when utter grief
Has darkened all hope of relief,
    And made our faith seem vain ;

And searchings into secrets hid
    For ever out of sight,
Translations of earth's pyramid,
And strife to raise the coffin lid,
    And pierce the distant night

Which closes life, but leaves behind
    A rope to reach the skies,
Tho' trembling fingers cannot find
The strands, and often we are blind
    To aught but the dead eyes,

And twine our minds in bondage strong
    With chain of golden hair ;
Forgetting, as we gaze along
The weary coming years, the wrong
    Will fade to silence there.

Ah merciful strong years ! how brave
    We learn to be from you !
How soon forgotten is the grave
O'er which the clinging grasses wave
    And mosses struggle thro' !

How small a wreath does memory weave
    Of all our anguish blooms ;
How calmly does our spirit leave
The thought behind, and rarely grieve
    O'er vanished sorrow's glooms!

Half bitterly my soul looks back
    To those same dropping tears,

Which left on my life's arid track
A little spot—the merest wrack
    On-dwelling thro' past years ;

But when they fell ; ah me, how deep
    The anguish they exprest ;
My heart sank down—I could but weep
And wish my sobs could ever steep
    My dead one's place of rest :

And yet my sorrow faded swift.
    What now remains to tell
The story of my life's one gift—
The star whose glow could well-nigh lift
    A lost soul out of hell—

The jewel which my mortal brow
    Let fall unwillingly
And never found again, yet how
It gleamed before, forgotten now,
    Or called back chillingly ?

A lock of hair whose golden hue
    Shines yet undimmed and bright,
As if the sunlight glinted thro'
And kissed it now, as I used to,
    And gloried in its light ;

A few old letters breathing still
    In fading dusty ink
The love which chained my ardent will,
And challenged death itself to kill,
    Or break the clasping link—

And yet 'tis broken ; or, could I,
　　Tho' sobbingly and low,
Speak of him here beneath the sky,
Or dream of grave where he doth lie,
　　And yet faint anguish know?

Sometimes I wondered in my pain
　　(Amid the dropping tears)
If peace indeed could bloom again—
If God were not a phantom vain,
　　And tragedies the years,

Whose heavy brows would never bow
　　On me their cooling breath ;
Alas, I know the presage now
Was but an empty doubt and vow
　　The coolness is of death.

I'd rather have my memories
　　Clear-cut against the black
Of daily life, than in strange eyes
See smiling love with mystic ties
　　Whose chains my hours lack !—

Let me recall the day gone by
　　(How little time it seems)
When first beneath the summer sky
I saw his face, nor marvelled why
　　He stepped from out my dreams :

Can my words paint him as he stood,
　　With sunlight falling fair

Around him, while from out the wood
Of pines, a whisper, understood
    Like music everywhere,

Came floating down the perfumed breeze,
    And tossing here and there
The waving rhythm of the trees
Till pale rose-petals on their knees
    Fell with a fragrant prayer ;

And he with calm eyes, saw not me
    At first, but gazed unmoved,
And knew a quiver, even he
Had marked not, till the hour when we
    Met ; and in meeting—loved.

I loved him with the untried might
    Of passion in my soul ;
I loved him as I loved the light
Returning to my craving sight
    As night away did roll :

All beauty, music, nobleness,
    I loved, as I loved him :
His lightest word could firm impress
The calmness of his stedfastness
    Upon my passing whim.

He cared not for the world's gay jest
    And rarely entered in,
But loved divinest music best,
And in her sweet tones found a rest
    Which light laugh could not win ;

And I loved best what he could choose,
    And music spoke to me
As none could speak ; nor did I lose
A shadow joy, and could refuse
    Content, all gaiety.

Ah love, it seems like yesterday
    That sunny time in June !
How swift the sunlight passed away,
And left a shadow where it lay,
    Like echo of love's tune.—

Alas, I wander, but recall
    My eyes, with tear-drops dim ;
I stood behind the garden wall,
Whose shadow o'er the road did fall
    Dreaming ; and so, saw him.

Men told me I was fair, and I
    Had (smiling half in scorn)
Oft in my child's heart wondered why ;
And gazed down blueness of the sky,
    And dreamed I was not born,

And marvelled if my fairness then
    Had shone out in a star ;
To blossom far beyond their ken,
Yet win like praises from these men,
    While I looked on afar ;

I knew, with that instinctive thrill
    Which moves a maiden's heart,

That they who wooed me could not fill
The depths of loving and of will,
    So held myself apart

From all their smiles, and tender eyes,
    And clasping fingers' touch ;
Love whispered of all mysteries,
Of rapture boundless as the skies,
    And here I found not such,

Until that sunny day behind
    The garden wall I stood,
Whose shadow stood out cool defined,
And thro' the white clouds golden-lined
    A breeze stole down the wood ;

And he passed by ; and all the air
    Fell chiming, wave on wave ;
I knew my fate, I felt it fair,
My dream's fulfilment met me there !
    Aye scoffers, you may rave,

First-sighted love may call a jest,
    Or out of fashion quite ;
But ah the souls who love the best
Wait not till wisdom crowns the rest
    Ere bathing in love's light !

My weak words hover (like a bird
    At drowsy close of day,
When scarce a passing leaf is stirred,
And thro' the sweetness dimly heard
    Her ' good-night ' floats away)

Around him ; and half fear to paint
    (For longing after sight)
My one lost love.  No crownèd saint,
With prayer and fasting waxing faint
    In dawning heaven's light,

Was he ; but just a man, and brave,
    And strong, and true, and free ;
Whose broad white brow a something grave,
The shadow of a bygone wave,
    Bore on its majesty ;

The sweetest eyes mine ever knew,
    With sunbeams prisoned there,
Dark grey, while ever peeping thro'
You caught a dash of heaven's blue
    In which star-raptures were ;

A mouth which smiled to meet the eyes,
    Yet closed firm in repose ;
Whose clear-cut lips would know not sighs
At any fate ; while calm and wise
    He stedfast plucked the rose

Although the thorns were piercing deep
    The human finger-tips,
Yet unmoved that the bloom would steep
Him sorrow full, he firm would keep
    That calm smile on his lips,

And know the gift God offered him,
    Tho' turning swift to woe,

A blessing bore beneath the rim
Of golden chalice, tho' so dim
    The light of love below,

That who sees not, will not believe
    The rich wine brimming there ;
And rather would men sigh and grieve
For that they have not, and bereave
    Their souls of faith so fair.

Oh mole-like in your platitudes,
    Ye little race of men,
Ye burrow 'mid your latitudes,
And know not any gratitudes
    For aught beyond your ken !

The boundless over-arching blue
    Of God's love o'er you cast—
The rapture star-lights shining thro'—
The glories hid in dropping dew—
    In present, and in past—

Would the poor mole who seeks the light
    And finds it darker still
Than burrowing below in night,
Which seems clear to his blinded sight
    And natural to his will,

Would he believe?  No; he would scorn,
    And call you dreamer then,
If you but hinted at the morn ;
And rather would he dwell forlorn,
    Than list your tale, oh men !

And mole-like are ye, oh most wise !
    God speaks so clear to you,
And still ye will not lift your eyes
To find revealings in the skies,
    So broad, and high, and blue.

Not such my love ; his soul drank deep
    In wisdom readily ;
Philosophy for him did steep
Her highest glory in calm sleep,
    But he gazed steadily

Beyond her slumbers to the end,
    And found in his own soul
A revelation, and a friend
Who half could the thick veiling rend
    Hiding the final goal.

He quaffed the poet's nectar cup
    At inspiration's spring,
And music bore his spirit up
Till his soul dare with angels sup,
    Borne on melodious wing.

And all men loved him, women too,
    And children most of all ;
They felt the glory shining thro'
The sweetness of his deep eyes' blue
    Where'er their glance did fall.

And I, his chosen, what felt I ?
    Alas ! how can I tell ?

How in hard words can make reply,
Or speak, or think, or reason why?
 Oh love, I loved thee well!

And yet not well enough, or thou
 Hadst rested here with me:
Oh love! my love! tho' tears drop now,
And furrowed is my once smooth brow
 With craving sore for thee—

Yet, had I loved thee, oh mine own,
 Could I live patiently
Without thee in the world alone,
With but a smothered sigh and moan
 To speak my agony?

Ah well! souls are so many-faced,
 And hold such different creeds;
And yet I say there is no waste
Of sweetness, and to every taste
 Is portioned what it needs.

A little of life's precious wine
 My youth drank from God's cup,
And held the chalice all divine
Round which love's roses thick did twine.
 And blooming, bore it up:

But when they faded, and a thorn
 Pressed in my heart abode,
To call to memory how forlorn
An even springs from fairest morn
 When sunshine only glowed;

Then, I could feel a Father's hand
    (And not an iron fate)
Was leading me through sorrow's land
To join my love amid the band
    Passing down heaven's gate.—

Our love grew with the summer hours,
    And 'mid the autumn's gold ;
The time passed like a dream of flow'rs,
And I thought happiness like ours
    Had never bloomed of old :

And one day as a silence fell
    From utter blissfulness
Upon my happy heart (how weil
Do I remember) he did tell
    Me of his first love's miss.

He was a boy, scarce twenty years
    Had crisped his golden hair ;
And she an orphan girl whose tears
He wiped away, and calmed her fears,
    And knew that she was fair ;

And gave the treasure of his love
    Into her trembling hand ;
Timid she was, a tender dove,
Whom angels called to bloom above,
    And leave her lover's land :

And so he lost her—ah how sweet
    His eyes looked into mine,

To kiss away a shade, or greet
The sunshine surging his to meet
    Behind the tear-drop's shine :

I felt no jealousy; ah no !
    My love pierced far too deep ;
And in the strength such passions know
I grudged her not that bitter woe
    Which once had made him weep :

And but drew closer to his side ;
    That he knew suffering,
And in grief's furnace had been tried,
And chosen once another bride,
    Bruised not my love's light wing.—

At last the ling'ring autumn swept
    Her glory far away,
And winter to her place swift stept,
While snow and ice the flowers kept
    Safe, till the spring woke gay ;

And when again the rose-leaves fell
    Adown the summer breeze,
And nightingales strove sweet to tell
The rapture which they knew so well,
    Amid the whisp'ring trees ;

And moon-fair breezes fluttered down
    The silver stars' deep light,
Whose beauty is the heaven's crown,
And bears the magic power to drown,
    By gazing with rapt sight,

All mortal anguish terror-strung
    On feeble human heart ;
My love said joy-bells should be rung
And clust'ring lily-garlands hung,
    And we no more should part.

Alas, for poor humanity
    So weak beneath the sun !
How swift the visions fair that we
Build up with dreams infinity
    To chaos only run !

Again the roses bloomed ; again
    The lilies budded fair ;
Again the earth with many a chain
Of woven blossoms, hill and plain
    Held fettered everywhere ;

Again the holy nightingale
    Beneath the mystic stars
Poured out her rapture down the vale,
And breathed again her last year's tale,
    And whispered of afars ;

But all the sweetness spoke to me,
    Who bore a lonely heart,
Of my past vanished ecstasy ;
For he, my love, was o'er the sea
    And we were still apart.

With the fair waking spring's first breath
    Of perfumed purple bloom

My love was called to meet stern death
Where war's fierce wave deep whispereth
   The highway to the tomb.

His country lay from mine apart
   A space of ocean tears,
But 'fatherland' dwelt in his heart
And bid him from my love depart—
   Ah bitter passing years,

Swift back ye roll !   Again I see
   His blue eyes as he pressed
One kiss upon my mouth, while he
Strove hard to murmur hopefully,
   And give my anguish rest :

'Sweetheart, beloved, I back return ;
   The laurel on my brow
Will with intenser glory burn
For every sigh thro' which I yearn
   In sorrow of the "now";

'Yet if, oh love, the winging death
   Shall strike me bitterly,
I'll bless thee with each passing breath,
And every tone that whispereth,
   And die in loving thee !'

We clung together ; hand in hand
   Close-grasping, till the pain
Which wrung our hearts could understand
The type of clasping fingers' band,
   And strike it back again :

Our lips met in a long embrace,
    Yet parted in despair,
While passion-pale shone out his face,
Grief's shadow blotting its fair grace
    Beneath his golden hair.—


My love !   My star !   the heightener
    Of wan life into bliss,
Whose kindling eye I would prefer
To even Christ the lightener
    (May God forgive me this !)


So left me in the summer-time,
    The happy time of flow'rs,
Whose fragrant bells a funeral chime
Seemed ringing with a mystic rime
    All thro' the dragging hours ;


And envious death, who marked afar
    My life-crown on my brow,
Strode cloud-enwrapped to dim my star,
And show what shadows mortals are
    Before whose pomp we bow !


What !   Do my tears drop down again
    So that I cannot speak ?
Has time then never healed the pain ?
I little thought in my disdain
    That I was half so weak ;


But speaking of the parting, brings
    My darling back to me ;

And every chord of mem'ry springs
Swift to its place, and wildly rings
    The bygone agony.—

Well; let it pass—I cannot tell
    How many years have flown,
Since he my love, who loved me well
Was killed; nor how the deed befell,
    For that was never known:

They found him when the fight was o'er
    Dead—dead—beneath the sky;
Ah God! (my heart is still so sore)
Is there no pity evermore?
    Is there no reason why?

No cause, that we a moment press
    With rapturous dim bliss
A glowing love with joy's excess,
And earth's vain dream of blessedness
    Held perfect in a kiss?

No cause, why we, to our wild heart
    A glory-image hold,
And holding, swift are struck apart,
Yet know not whence the stinging dart
    Came winging, hard and cold?

There is no answer—save a sigh
    From every human soul;
We feel our destiny is high—
We feel we have a helper nigh—
    We strive to grasp a whole,

R

And find a fragment in our hand,
    A fragile silver thread,
Whose end we cannot understand—
A fragile thread—a broken strand—
    And all we know—is said.—

Oh love ! my love ! thy calm dead eyes
    Bore no reproach, or tear ;
But mutely gazed to the blue skies ;
And still that smile so sweet and wise
    Thy lips held firm and clear :

So much they told me ; oh my love,
    That face still haunts my sight !
I gaze on earth, I gaze above,
And know nor faith, nor hope, nor love,
    Nor glow, nor joy, nor light,

Save in those eyes, which shadow me
    In blissful heaven-calm.
When shall I feel the ecstasy
Of clasping hands again with thee
    With no death to alarm ?

'Twas long ago, as men count time
    By days, and months, and years ;
But still my mind serene can climb
Life's ladder to the rhythmic chime
    Of stars—thro' falling tears.

*Spottiswoode & Co., Printers, New-street Square, London.*

www.ingramcontent.com/pod-product-compliance
Lightning Source LLC
Chambersburg PA
CBHW020104030726
47498CB00006B/1941